CLOSE, TOO CLOSE

CLOSE, TOO CLOSE

The Tranquebar Book of Queer Erotica

Edited by

MEENU AND SHRUTI

TRANQUEBAR

TRANQUEBAR PRESS
An imprint of westland ltd
Venkat Towers, 165, P.H. Road, Maduravoyal, Chennai 600 095
No. 38/10 (New No.5), Raghava Nagar, New Timber Yard Layout, Bangalore 560 026
Survey No. A-9, II Floor, Moula Ali Industrial Area, Moula Ali, Hyderabad 500 040
23/181, Anand Nagar, Nehru Road, Santacruz East, Mumbai 400 055
4322/3, Ansari Road, Daryaganj, New Delhi 110 002

First published in TRANQUEBAR by westland ltd 2012

10 9 8 7 6 5 4 3 2 1

ISBN: 978-93-81626-15-3

Typeset in Palatino Linotype by SÜRYA, New Delhi
Printed at Manipal Technologies Ltd., Manipal

Contents

Ark Erotica   endpapers
Anirban Ghosh

Foreword   vii
Vikram Doctor

Introduction   xi

Pity that Blush   1
Annie Dykstra

Dreams and Desire in Srinagar   15
Michael Malik G.

Perfume   31
D'Lo

Jewel and the Boy   47
Abeer Hoque

Give Her A Shot   64
Msbehave

Soliloquy   87
Chicu

Shadowboxer 97
  Nilofer

The Marriage of Somavat and Sumedha 109
  Devdutt Pattanaik

All in the Game 121
  Iravi

The Half Day 141
  Doabi

Upstairs, Downstairs 153
  Nikhil Yadav

Conference Sex 173
  Ellen L.R.

I Hate Wet Tissues 184
  Satya

Screwing with Excess 193
  Vinaya Nayak

Contributors 211
Acknowledgements 215

Foreword

Vikram Doctor

Vikram Doctor is a journalist based in Mumbai where he writes on food and gay issues. He is involved with the group Gay Bombay (www.gaybombay.org).

While browsing among the few booksellers that still cling to Mumbai's pavements, if you dig below their piles of Mills & Boons novels, self-help books and the accumulated works of Chetan Bhagat, you will often come across American pulp novels from the '60s and '70s. Most of these have covers featuring macho men and barely-clad women along with weapons, cars and piles of cash, but just occasionally the covers will show two men, or two women, and in positions that suggest they have more than playing chess in mind.

Titles like *When Love Must Hide, The Strange Women* and *Journey to Eros* make it clear that they are examples of same-sex erotica that made their way to India at a time when an anthology like this could hardly have been imagined. I find these books oddly compelling, not for their lurid artwork and variable writing, but as signs of gay and lesbian life from past decades in Mumbai, when it may have been relatively repressed, but yet stubbornly endured.

It is true, of course, that such lesbian erotica was often written and read by men looking for a different kind of titillation, but there is always the possibility that some women may have found it here and recognised feelings within themselves that they might not have otherwise articulated. 'It is through desire that many people first know of their sexuality', write the editors of this anthology, and this is where erotica becomes a catalyst in helping you articulate what might have otherwise remained unacknowledged, even unnameable. Even those men getting turned on by the ladies, while hardly signs of a conventional queer sensibility, still unwittingly provide evidence of how sexual attractions can fall beyond the normative heterosexual frame.

The stories collected here provide ample evidence of such non-normative attractions, not just gay and lesbian, but bisexual and even beyond the simply sexual, as with Satya's story of a transman's desire which goes to a more essential, bodily level. There is also the woman in Doabi's story who wonders at the end whether the sex was better than the bowl of rajma her lover has just fed her, and if this seems flippant, you haven't tasted how satisfying a bowl of rajma – a recipe is helpfully provided – can be!

That rajma is also proof of how these attractions are expressed in specifically South Asian terms. This is rarer than it might seem. The one thing that hasn't changed from those days of American pulp erotica is how we still seem to take our overt sexual stimulation from abroad. Indirect stimulation abounds of course, from Bollywood bromances to girls acting 'tomboy' on Indian reality TV shows, but actual South Asian erotica or porn has tended to be too depressingly sleazy to allow for any real appreciation (and when it just might, it is soon shut down – as with the Savita Bhabi strips).

There is real pleasure then in reading of desires couched in specifically familiar terms, and interest too – I had never considered the erotic possibilities of sari pleats until reading D'Lo's story of the seduction of a school teacher! The rhythms of traditional story-telling used by Devdutt Pattanaik for his tale of Somavat and Sumedha may seem subversive, down to its amusedly voyeuristic cow, until you remember the uninhibited spirit that runs through so much Indian folklore and mythology, unquenched by the prudery often imported, like those pulp novels, from abroad.

Pulp, in fact, is always an adjunct to prudery, and the fact that a collection like this, which is the opposite of pulp, can come out openly is a hopeful sign of how we might be moving beyond prudery as well. But if by this, browsing book buyer, you are expecting a raunchy read, think again. The stories here might be explicit, but they largely avoid the prurient spirit of pure porn. They are, of course, erotic, which means they deal also with the subtleties of suggestion, the explorations of eye-contact, the imaginations and recollections of intimacy, rather than merely with full, fleshy details.

Don't put this book down in disappointment, though, because its pleasures are real, and rarer. Porn, after all, is available with a few clicks, but the erotic has become harder to find. The stories here present it in different styles and settings, showing how it can creep into the drawing rooms of Nikhil Yadav's and Vinaya Nayak's stories, which mix social satire with sex, as well as into the humdrum bus ride of Chicu's story, where the protagonist, who fears what a surprising revelation might bring, is surprised in turn by the response she gets.

That story also illustrates how this anthology differs from so much other queer writing. The genre has been dominated by a few narratives, such as that of coming out and of the violence, loss and shame this often brings. This collection is refreshingly free from these. Violence is displaced by attraction responded to, or even just calm acceptance – as in Michael Malik's story set in Kashmir which shows something rare in queer fiction, though perhaps more common in real life than we imagine: the acknowledgement of attraction, but an equal acceptance of different realities where queer and straight worlds meet.

It is an adult story in the real sense, and eroticism is an adult emotion, not made 'for adults-only' in the sense of the x-rated, but made by adults encountering and accepting the possibilities and limits of attraction. This is an adult anthology, enjoy it that way.

Introduction

Meenu and Shruti

When we pick up a book of erotica, what magic does it hold for us? It may excite us, arouse us, perhaps even pique our curiosity. The appeal of erotica lies in its ability to capture our sexual imagination, in the promises it holds of pleasures and possibilities. It is to this appeal of erotic possibility that we hope to speak in this anthology, as we present contemporary literature about queer sex lives, erotic experiences and passions. This book is an attempt to explore the less visible zones of queer sex writing from South Asia and bring it into the public domain, thereby making queer lives apparent in compelling new ways.

It is through desire that many people first know of their sexuality. In most cultures, sexual expression is seen as valid only if it is contained within heterosexual, married, monogamous set-ups. What then becomes of people whose desires mark them as different, whose stirrings are turned into a pledge of silence? A lifetime could go by without even knowing that the pleasure one seeks is also sought by many others. Every day, people are living sexual lives that step outside the normative, but their lives and stories are usually kept secret or hidden. The shame and silence accompanying their desire makes sure that normative sexuality remains unquestioned. Given this context, we as queer feminists believe it is critical to work towards a world where all sexualities can be equally expressed, where non-normativity, fluidity and multiplicity is abundant. This is what we understand as queer – a perspective and political identity that confronts the heteronormative ideal[1] and the respectability it offers. For us, queerness knocks down the assumption that everyone is heterosexual and shifts the notion that only two genders, fixed at birth on the basis of biology, exist. Instead, queer foregrounds sexual and gender diversity and celebrates the plurality of sexualities, genders, sexual expressions and lived realities.

Five years ago, the two of us – queer women hunting for erotica that reflected our desires – could only find published queer erotica written in and about the west. Maybe we didn't know where to look, but to us it felt like there wasn't enough contemporary erotica that reflected non-western contexts in general or the culture-specificity of our lives in particular. Queer sexual voices and writings have of course always existed but have been shared in more private, intimate

---

[1]'rigid notions of what it means to be man or woman, how the two should relate and the family unit that should result from such a relationship. All those who dare to think outside the perfect ideal are considered threats to "morality" and to society at large.' *Because I Have A Voice: Queer Politics in India*. Narrain and Bhan (eds). 2005. Yoda Press, pg. 3.

settings. Dirty stories have been swapped orally but perhaps not been made available in the public sphere. More recently, things have been changing in terms of the expression of queer sexual lives within the South Asian region. Autonomous zines like *Scripts*[2] and *Chay*[3], blogs like Gaysi[4] and Allygator Lover[5], collectives like Nigah[6] and smaller groups having BDSM-specific conversations, have all been expanding the spaces available to read, write and talk sex. Over the years, we have engaged with these spaces, with feminist movements and queer rights work in India. Editing this anthology is another attempt at foregrounding queer sexual voices by inviting people to share hidden, simmering queer erotic writing.

---

[2]SCRIPTS is a zine published at least once a year by LABIA (Lesbians and Bisexuals in Action). It is a vibrant space for multiple conversations of queer/feminist/activist/creative voices. www.labiacollective.org

[3]Having observed in Pakistani society, a disturbing tendency towards fear and shame around issues of sex and sexuality – that is to say, around a normal human interaction – the founders of Chay Magazine feel that sex and sexuality should enter the public discourse. http://chaymagazine.org

[4]Gaysi Family was started to provide a voice and a safe space to desis who identify as LGBT. What began as a simple idea of sharing stories about what it meant to be gay and desi (gaysi!) has evolved into a space full of traffic from around the world. http://gaysifamily.com

[5]One of the first Indian erotic blogs we came across: allygatorlover.blogspot.com. A blog, self-descriptively, about homo-sex!

[6]Literally 'perspective' in Urdu/Hindi, Nigah begins and furthers conversations, thoughts, debates, diatribes, rants, plays, art, protests, hissy fits and any other form of expression on issues of gender and sexuality. nigahdelhi.blogspot.com

As queers, many of us definitely want to talk about pleasure, about orgasms, fantasies and earth-shattering sex. We enjoy sex and are not ashamed of it. The rules of normative sexuality don't apply to us yet (. . . or so we hope) and this often challenges the way sex is usually understood. We confront, redefine, dispute and reclaim what sex is. If we subvert the norm, it frees us and we learn to pleasure ourselves in newer ways. The transgressive nature of queer perspectives and lives lends itself to much diversity, which we hoped the stories in this anthology would reflect. We wanted this anthology to be varied and inclusive of many sexual expressions, and from multiple gender and sexuality viewpoints. In short, we imagined this anthology to be queer and not necessarily only lesbian or gay or bi or trans erotica.

To start the process, we sent out an open call for submissions to queer lists, literary groups and blogs in India and the South Asian diaspora globally. Other than India, we were able to reach out to groups and individuals from Bangladesh, Nepal, Pakistan and Sri Lanka that engage with queer rights, writings and art. We also invited some published authors and artists to contribute to this anthology. And then, we waited with baited breath. As the stories began to trickle in, they exceeded our expectations. The stories we eventually chose expand some of the traditional notions that exist about sex: in private, between two people only and within a relationship. In these pages, you will find sex taken into the public arena – into changing rooms and public transport; sexual games between guests at a party and a threesome; and no-strings-attached sex as well as one night stands that are not tied into a relationship set-up. We did not choose stories simply because they were explicit, but selected ones that capture a range of the emotions that the sexual can elicit. The stories here are sexy, dirty, cheeky, dark, intriguing, sizzling and haunting. We chose certain stories because they complicated the notion of consent. We believe that consent is critical; for us, erotica has consent enmeshed with it. While 'no means no' and coercion is out of line, what yes means can be a tricky matter, very subjective and sometimes negotiated in murky ways. Consent cannot be black and white and some stories in this book explore that grey zone in between. Finally, we were delighted to find a graphic story that embellishes the book beautifully, the artist's strokes depicting thoughts, dreams and pleasure. Given the diversities of queer realities, we cannot claim to have been representative. There are complexities of class, language, genders, sexual acts, age, abilities, subjective experiences, regions and different bodies that cannot be encompassed within one book nor packed into one box. This anthology is peppered with stories that reflect just a slice of our myriad realities.

The coming pages offer our readers a kaleidoscope of lust, yearning and passion. This evocative selection was made possible thanks to our contributors. There is no doubt that many people write erotica, often intensely intimate, sometimes shared with only a lover or kept entirely hidden. Sharing it, whether by reading it or writing it, may expose you or put you under judgement, so it is difficult to disclose. Boldly picking a book of erotica off the shelf, reading erotica openly and talking about it are all powerful acts. We raise a toast to each of you who have engaged with erotica.

Now, gear up for a good read. *Close, Too Close* is going to leave you horny and thrilled, perhaps puzzled or even disturbed, aroused, satiated or craving. It's erotica with an edge and we hope it inspires you to keep seeking more.

Meenu and Shruti
Bombay 2012

Pity that Blush

Annie Dykstra

Struggling with the drawstring on the bag that held my goggles and swimming costume, I walk from the car park to the Club pool, pulled only by the anticipation of my resulting self-righteousness.

The pool buildings glow a little. Low slung and harsh. Fronted by ridiculous Doric columns. Opened 75 years ago for British civil servants. The rules upon rules still hung fast. The membership was still so exclusive that people hardly looked at each other. I follow the deep stench of chlorine as it curls up through the sausage tree fruits. The pool entrance is hidden deep away from the road. I think about wonderful evenings sitting alone on the lawn, watching the bats leap out from the tree with the moon behind. Disturbed fruit, as I walk below.

~

The changing room attendant takes great interest in forcing me to wear a cap and place my clothes and bag as they should be.

On the bench.

I had complained that my hair was short enough but she insisted. Even I could not argue with her. The cap aches my forehead. Pulls single hairs sadistically and tightens the newly-shaven sides. Makes my forearm hair alert to the Delhi winter morning chill.

~

The door to the pool clangs open begrudgingly to show hurried solitary swimmers. The morning was always hurried and alien. On Saturday afternoons the children forced more humanity. But pre-work length swimming meant no unnecessary chat with the attendant and no eye contact with other swimmers, allowing me to meditate throughout. Self flagellation before 9 a.m.: it always suited my bad-tempered introversion. The Calvinist changing room with its prison doors, cold concrete and complicated locker arrangements only accentuated my ugly Attica mood. Pulling on my cold still-damp costume appealed to my morning masochism. I can see the others rubbing sleep out of their eyes before stretching goggles tightly over them. Targeted pink rings will be an all-day reminder of our mutual surrender.

I unroll the sticky costume over my body, admiring the tone that these swims have given to my arms. A smooth curve has appeared on the underside of my upper arm, sweeping down to my elbow, new muscles standing proud. My back is now a careful separation of units of strength and I always glance at how my Speedo straps stand taller than my muscles. The material pulls away from my firm skin, denying the lycra a closer fit. As I pull the costume over my nipples, the cool lifts them proud into the black matte costume and I realise that a lack of late-night fucking has left my body angry and edgy with the injustice. She dared to deny me last night.

~

Entering the water's tunnel swiftly and neatly, I begin the long smooth underwater stokes to warm up. I ease through the water watching the sunlight begin to sparkle the pool floor. My bubbles of breath catching light at one particular end of the pool. Ducking hard at each end, my forehead tucking down to release the kick from the ball of my foot. Feeling the water bubble through my nostrils and thoughts slipping through them. The rhythm of lengths upon lengths. Thinking of nothing but breath and rolling strokes. I'm starting to enjoy the ache in my arms, knowing that they pull my body, knowing I'm fast and sleek in the water. It takes me a while to notice.

You are swimming breaststroke in front of me, fast but elegant. I slide past you a couple of times smoothly and you keep the same speed as me, steadily slipping your way back and forth. I can make out only a tightly-wound ponytail tied carefully away, making a smooth bump under the rubber cap. I wonder how that hair looks around your shoulders, behind your head as you lie flat on the pillow with eyes closed. But now, below the water, I study your rounded body with intense interest. Purposefully slowing down behind you, I tip to the right and plunge further into front crawl and gaze as your legs part, then come together. Your bum is lean and firm. Your breasts sharply come back to your body. Your stomach is flat. You are fit. There is no ripple in the skin tone. Just large, strong legs tidily sloping into a round bum with a small dimple on either side. I watch your costume ride up as you swim more and more. The elastic edges dig into the darker skin around the top of your thighs, making the dents look blue on your brown skin. Water does strange things to skin tone. Your browner skin looks lightly blue, my paler skin looks yellow. There are goose bumps on the top of your arms as you warm up. Your costume is a cute white polka dot on blue. In the pool it is hard to read the clues of butch and femme, but now I have enough. I'm following a fit, strong, long-haired femme. My long investigation from behind you over these few laps has moved from lazy lusty gazing to active stalking.

As you stop to rest at the pool end, I tumble turn, trying to remain cool. Your elbows are propped up in the pool's shelf. Your cleavage sits just under the water's edge. I stare at the costume's cups holding your breasts at just the right angle. I catch sight of a red glow on your cleavage. I love your boldness in wearing that low-cut costume here. I toy with the idea of talking to you, but lose the nerve. I hope we are playing pool tango.

~

I rush to swim off the thoughts in my head and the horniness that creeps into me. Why now, here, so early in the morning? This will ruin me for the day. There will be nowhere to wank, here at the club or at work. I try to focus on the work I have to do and people I am meeting for lunch, but again find myself behind you as you launch yourself forward inappropriately in front of my face and into my track on the next lap.

This time, as I see your legs open and close, I glimpse a slip of you escaping from your costume. A tip of lighter lip escaping. Completely mesmerized and stricken. I am a rabbit caught in the headlights wanting to jump to the safety of the hedge, but unable to, I plough on behind you, slowing my pace, my goggle eyes widening to focus on the soft tone of your pussy. You are shaved. I love that neatness. It means that your costume slips more smoothly over your lips. I peer forward to see how far up your costume rides as you kick out. I stare at the cross hatching on the elastic trenches that frame your lips. But you kick too fast to let me see inside. Now I really want you.

~

Eventually you push yourself out of the pool using your arms and, with a quick flip, you are up on your feet. You don't look back. Swing your hips. Brazen femme you are. I'm devastated. You slip away to the changing rooms. I try to exorcise my energy by swimming four laps of front crawl, powerfully pounding the pool and breathing deeply. Trying to hold back some cool before I slither after you.

However, before finishing my usual fifty, I lose my nerve and creep sheepishly back to the changing rooms. Suddenly hoards of women are changing and rubbing and oiling and giggling inside. The Lodi estate madams have arrived, their children being driven to school as they get changed. Time on their side, they are discussing the newest members. Usually I slip into the corner to avoid feeling like a voyeur and unexpected guest in their assumed sexless zone. This time I relish the play and the opportunity to look from body to body to search you out. One woman catches my gaze roaming the scores of half-naked bodies and tightens her eyes. I'm breaking the changing room code. Cruising at the club. My father will at some point be told. Politely, on the balcony or when he recommends a new member. He puts up with a lot. The lifted eyebrows of the tennis ladies when I wear my favourite ribbed vests and button-fly jeans. The low rumble of tut-tut across the lawns when I come here with my rapid succession of fuck buddies. The way I hold my cigarettes. How I'm too friendly with the waiters.

~

But my arousal has pushed me into this reckless mood. I linger on the soft curves of one of the more aloof Lodi madams. I pause at a swimmer rubbing a rough towel across her back. One tall athletic figure has surprisingly cropped hair. I thought I was the only one. She pulls her costume down her broad shoulders and I gaze at her large dark nipples in the mirror. At least two inches wide, with an almost black tone gradually easing into wheatish skin. Her breasts barely contain them.

Finally I see you, disappeared into a corner. Your costume is still on. Your body looks stronger as you stand up. I carefully move my towel and bag next to where you are changing, any shyness dissolved by lust. Did you glance at me? And why was your costume still on? Could I dare to guess you are undressing slowly for my benefit?

I start to get my clothes ready and dry my hair roughly.

I can gaze at you from under my towel. You turn, and look at me with a start. I wonder if you recognize me. You seem to, and I see your gaze slip to my arms and now even more alert nipples.

~

I peel my costume off and start to slowly rub myself dry, feeling strong and confident, the neat lines of my body on show.

Then you peel the edges of your costume off and I can see the lines where the elastic has marked your soft skin. A white zigzag on your shoulders and around the edge of your breasts. Looking at me, you edge your polka-dot costume down your flat stomach. Your breasts spring out of it. I can see your back in the mirror. As your arms pull your costume down your body, the definition of your back muscles becomes stronger. I can see the strength of your back and softness of your breasts both at the same time. The mirror-covered wall has never been so welcome. The constant clanging of the pool doors is muffled as I'm getting lost in you. Momentarily I think of the strict attendant, but now I'm in the tunnel of no return watching you from every side.

I'm beyond caring as you stand naked before me. You catch my gaze and follow it back boldly, although I catch a flash of timidity on your eyelids and a slight rising of your breasts. They are magnificent, large and deep with a close line of cleavage and dark, dark small nipples. Smooth and upright, they rest on your taut stomach which lies flat until the front of your thighs. You look even stronger than you did in the water. You face me and I start to put cream on my arms. I have pulled my costume hurriedly to the floor. The moist of me mixing with the moist of pool. I stuff the costume back past the drawstring. Force my hand with a push past the top knot. My thumb caught outside the string.

But now both of us are naked. Obvious that now we are together in this.

I offer you some cream on my upturned hand, with a smile but no words. My nails, thankfully, I cut yesterday. I see you studying my hand. It's strong and sometimes too wide. You take the cream and, carefully, whilst still watching me, rub it into your breasts one at a time. I can feel your eyes on my eyes as I gaze at you softly caressing cream across, around your nipples. A small dash is left just at their highest point.

I back into the shower cubicle. The curtain is just wide enough to fill the space. The cold tiles on the back wall make me gasp as I lean against them. I wait for a second to see if you will follow me in. You do. I see two of the other women lift an eyebrow together to wonder. The changing room attendant stares, confused.

As you close the curtain behind you, I lift one creamed hand and place it on your right breast, feeling the nipple between finger and thumb and rolling it in my hand. I see your goose bumps extend across your cleavage and up your neck. As you bite your lip to stop a gasp from escaping I roll your nipple between finger and thumb sweetly at first, then with a tightness that surprises you. I enjoy watching your eyes quiz me as I pinch your nipple between finger and thumb. I turn you around to press against the back of the cubicle. You fall back onto the tiled wall, making a quiet thud with the back of your head.

I push my hands underneath your breasts, squeezing them together to feel their full weight. Your eyes close and your gasps are suppressed by the force of my clenched teeth and my lips on yours.

I start to imagine the pinkness inside you and feel the rapid desire to push into you rise in me. I bite your neck, push closer and closer up into your ear, smelling the wet chlorine and tasting edges of hair. I can feel the warmth of the fast swim and desire in you. I bite so hard your knee kicks out against my thigh but I stop that by pressing my body into yours and pushing the length of you against the wall, marking your neck with a dotted pink half-moon from my teeth.

My breath is rapid and heavy. Yours mirrors mine. I clasp your hands in mine behind you and pull your arms. Bend onto your nipples. Pull your arms together behind you, so I can clench into your soft bouncy flesh. I leave a trail of matching teeth prints zigzagging across your tits. I enjoy the slow, even, methodical process of marking you. Turn you into a treasure trail.

~

I turn the shower on. Take one of my hands away from you to hold your hair. As I guessed, it's long, down to your shoulders. I grasp all of it in one hand, tighten my grip and pull your head back. Now I just look at you. You move your gaze from the ceiling to me. Look up at me from under your eyelids. I finalize the bites with a nip on your earlobe. Then whisper, 'Say "more".'

You are silent. I knew you were strong. So I start to loosen my grip on hair and arms. Start to pull my body away from yours. Pull out of the long tunnel of lust back into chlorine stench and damp towels.

'More,' you finally growl with less meekness than I expected.

So, I turn on the shower. Push you down onto your knees. Hold your hair again into the stream. Then your face. Watching the water wash over your eyes. Into your mouth.

I lean into the shower and pull you onto me. You stumble, shocked, surprised at the order of things, but quickly catch up. I part my legs and pull the roughness of your cold tongue into me. Now hungry, you graze over me through the water and spray. Licking carefully around me. Managing to tease me. I push and pull you where I want you. Pull you out of me when it gets too much. Frustrate you. Then smash your face back into my cunt, hard. I sit on your face to make you look at me as your tongue enters me. But I'm not giving you too much. I love watching your startled face as I let the water drain over it. But I love more the willingness you have to kneel and how you hold still whilst the shower pounds your forehead, closes your eyes and runs off your nose.

Now ravenous, I pull up, push you against the wall and drop onto my knees and face your stomach. My hands occupied with your hands, I have only my head to explore with. Again, the beauty of the flat muscles reaching up and under your breasts takes me by surprise. The perfect straight line above your belly button. I use your hands to clasp your bum and pull you, with you, onto my face.

With a second to hold still and contemplate the scene, I gather my breath, readying myself. Dazed by what I had managed to accomplish. Limp in my arms you are waiting for me. How quickly this had all happened.

~

I push my chin against you, feeling you wet, and slip myself between your legs. I let go of your arms but you still hold them behind your back. That suits me, I don't want any distractions, don't want you to touch me. I hold you steady as I pull your legs apart. Pointing my tongue, I carefully touch your clit with the mere tip.

Shaking now, your legs are easing apart, begging me to move further in. I gaze at the glistening pinkness of you, inside. Remembering the stolen glimpses of you escaping from your costume, how I had followed you from the lengths of the pool to here some many moons ago, I hold my hands under you and ease my face up and under you.

Now all of you is available to me. I run my tongue lengthways up and down you. Warmth moves from me to you. I taste the pool in you. You are so wet I cannot feel you. You move your leg onto the shower tap, high in the cubicle, widening yourself to me, willing me into you. I want to hold back. But cannot. Pressing your lips apart, I look at you. Red eases into pink and I can see the full you. Smooth and clean and shaven, your colours are open to me.

I turn you around quickly and you gather your balance by pressing against the wall, your face squashed flat against the tiles. I push your leg back up onto the wooden bench as you sway from side to side. Then I lay my hand flat against you.

I start to work myself into you, one finger at a time. I can slip into you easily. You open up to me so quickly. The warmth shocks me. My hands are cold from the changing room and swim. My fingers are encased and numb within seconds. Relief starts to spread through me and I can start to concentrate on listening to your breathing and feeling you from inside.

I am looking up into you and watching my fingers disappear and reappear. You start to push greedily onto me. Angry. Wanting. I start to chart the waves of pleasure pushing and pulling you in and out of letting go. The ups and downs of the laps. Meditating on you. I stand behind you and muffle your sighs with my other hand. I don't want us to have to leave now.

We are building up a cycle of pleasure that I control. I like the occasional sound of other showers being turned on, lockers being closed. I stand up, take my costume and pull your hands behind your back and make the elastic hold them tightly. I harshly tie my speedo tightly around your hands and them tight against your back. I am biting your wet hair, pulling small strands with my teeth. I cautiously chart your pleasure against my own.

I have you now.

You are starting to buckle under me. With relief. Your knees suddenly weak. I'm holding the weight of you now. You are helpless with erotic charge and trapped with my speedo.

And now I want this finished. Without talking. No exchange.

I want to shower, get to work and be gone.

I want to quickly stop being lost. To come back to earth. Not to be responsible for your desire. Harshly, I move more quickly in and out of you. You are squealing, wiggling, buckling on my hand. I'm surprised by my own breathing, by the hard work. At last you squeak your final muffled cry and we feel a breaking of this pressure.

I can't get away quickly enough.

~

The awkwardness of leaving the cubicle. Rushing for the shower curtain. The light blush that rises up your throat and through your face. Trying to look for a connection.

You start to speak. Open your mouth and close it again. I know you want to make this safe in your way. They all do. Or want to give it a verbal future. It's the yearning that spoils it. I look away.

Her denial last night has been your undoing today.

I leap out of the shower. Without looking up, I know the attendant is watching. I scour myself with the towel. Pull the hard pile across my back and legs. Squash my damp towel back into the into my drawstring bag, harshly pushing it through the string.

~

I take one look back. You are calmly creaming your legs. You look up direct into my eyes. You try to bounce my mercy back at me. Then, tip your right eyebrow at me but I recognize that look of yearning.

~

I can see a blush rising. I pity it.

Hurriedly, I swoop back across the now warm lawns. Head down into the street through the crowds of schoolchildren. Jump quickly into a rickshaw. He pulls sideways out into the relief of the busy road. My thoughts move easily to my first coffee of the day.

Dreams and Desire in Srinagar

Michael Malik G.

To escape the flames of Delhi in May for the hills is to leave hell for heaven, and even dirty and congested Shimla feels heavenly that time of year. But this May I was heading further north to Srinagar, to see Mahmood. It would be my second trip to Kashmir, but the first time I'd see him on his home turf. We met a few years back during a gaydar moment, a double-take while passing one another on the Corniche in Doha, where he runs a shop selling Indian textiles in one of the bazaars and waits for summer and his yearly trip back home. We hit it off immediately that first scorching Qatari afternoon, when we had memorable conversations that were his initiation to the novel idea that one could be gay *and* be happy and proud. He's swung through Delhi on his way home each year since, to spend a couple of days at a time with me, mostly in my bed.

I guess poor Mahmood's been in love with me since that first day. He goes into small depressions each time we part. He's a good man, not bad looking, the right age (thirty-plus), and he's great sex. I like him plenty, but the love thing, sadly, never fell into place for me. It's a familiar theme that runs through my long, bungled relationship history: liking a chap, a few intensely, but still never *enough* to go all the way and walk confidently into the future with him by my side. Mahmood brushed off my regret for coming up short as unnecessary. We'd be friends, with benefits. Though wounded, he put up a brave front.

~

Three Octobers ago, on the first trip to Kashmir, I'd landed quite accidentally on the ramshackle houseboat of seventeen-year-old Shahid, after finding that the boat I'd originally reserved was being waterproofed and reeked of brain-crushing fumes. His father deceased, Shahid was the teenage man of the family, taking care of his mother, three elder sisters, the houseboat business, all while going to school. He was born on the boat and had spent all his life on the boat. His family's only social contacts were with other boat families. It's a thick culture. Two of his sisters were to be married to men who also live on the lake, in a double wedding that was certain to be financially ruinous. Shahid said they would need 400 kilos of meat for several hundred guests because after eating everyone was supposed to take home meat. I'm vegetarian and I shuddered when I heard that.

That October, for three days Shahid didn't leave my side. I'm a passionate traveler and a very independent one at that, so I politely resisted the violation of my freedom at first, but when he insisted that it was his duty to take care of me, a man more than twenty-five years his senior, I was charmed. It didn't take long for me to like him, platonically of course. It would be easy enough to dream up Kashmiri affection and hospitality as a different kind of intention, especially if the one offering it is a handsome and athletic young man and the one receiving it is me. I didn't think he was gay or even bi, but even if he was, my personal hands-off policy toward the under-eighteen crowd is non-negotiable, no matter how cute, smart, or sexy, and Shahid was all of that.

After my return to Delhi he kept in touch with regular phone messages. Before long, he was writing that I should have a profile on Facebook like everyone else, counsel I had resisted successfully from others in the past. He said we could be *friends* there, though I thought we were friends already. Like that, I became a reluctant, but never-to-turn-back social networker. Shahid found me and we were connected. In every SMS and Facebook chat over three years I could count on two questions aside from *how r u*. One was when I was coming back to Kashmir. What I couldn't figure out was whether it was my company he sought, or business for the boat. We did have three good days together, crisscrossing Nagin Lake in cushioned and canopied shikaras, taking pictures with the flowers in Shalimar Gardens, and walking the mountains above Gulmarg. But his family also needed guests. The wedding took place last year. They were probably broke.

The other dependable chat question was when I was getting married. I usually answered with a crisp *not yet*, which wasn't a lie, but one day the moment arrived when I decided I wasn't going to be asked that anymore, and I told Shahid that if and when I did get married, it would be to a man. Maybe it was risking a parting of ways, but I was out across the board everywhere else in my life. That I would continue to withhold this basic fact of my existence from someone who was no longer a kid at twenty, and supposedly my friend, stopped making sense to me. I reasoned that he should learn something about the world beyond the lake. So I threw the dice and let the chips fall as they may. His reply, a wish that I have a happy life with whomever I wanted to be with, astonished me because faulty belief in my vast and superior experience had me convinced that I'd already heard it all, and that no surprises were left. I thanked him for the wish.

The follow-up surprise was a repeated enquiry as to when I was coming to Kashmir, which in light of my disclosure, sounded different to me this time. I told him that indeed I had a trip planned for the end of May, and without pause he told me I'd stay on the boat. Disappointed that I'd already made plans with another friend in Srinagar, I offered to stay on the boat my first day and join my friend on the second. Mahmood wasn't going to like that.

Once offline, nagging questions bounced around my head. How could it be that he, a young Kashmiri of traditional upbringing, was that open-minded? From where would that have come? Shahid knows I'm gay and *still* asks for me on the boat? Was something else stirring in his mind? Could it be? That maybe *he*? No. He hadn't given any clues. I chided myself for falling into the common cynicism among too many folks in our queer society that gay-friendly straights must have underhanded motives or desire us clandestinely. I despised that thinking. It wasn't me. Maybe too much time around shady and opportunistic guys in Delhi had misshapen my beliefs. But no, I had to take responsibility for my own jaded attitudes. Shahid was simple, and just good.

But my principles called foul. Gay is good too. That was one of the mantras of the pride movement, so why couldn't that apply to Shahid? What if questions of sexuality were indeed stirring within him? If so, then surely he wanted me as a role model who would help him understand who he was. But that bothered me too. Oddly, I felt myself protecting him. But from whom? From others who might hurt him? From me? The question disturbed me. I don't do kids. But Shahid wasn't a kid, not anymore. He was a young man, and old enough to make choices and decisions that were his own. I tossed these bothersome thoughts aside, but knew they would come running back for me for at the end of May.

I called Mahmood. As expected, he wasn't happy with the change of plans. Neither did he appreciate my narration of the online chat with Shahid. I told him not to sweat, that Shahid was most probably straight but open-minded, to his credit. Mahmood thought it strange. I told him to put his hand into his pocket and start playing ball, because we were going to mate like rabbits the minute we could get behind a locked door. That turned his mood around.

During the month before my arrival at Srinagar, Shahid sent messages and caught me several times on Facebook's live chat. He wrote that he was excited to see me again. He also wrote that we would have *fun*. I always stumble over that loaded word, and felt myself flush.

Mahmood picked me up at the airport and half an hour later we were out on a rowboat. We spotted Shahid in the distance on the rear deck of his houseboat. As we approached and got a clearer view, there was no denying that the boy of seventeen had filled out nicely into a hunk. I like hands and I remember them, sometimes even better than faces. A hand that was larger and rougher than I remembered reached down for mine and helped me up. Mahmood followed without assistance. Shahid greeted us with handshakes, an open palm over the heart, and a wide smile. No longer the simple kid of the first visit, he now seemed in command of his surroundings.

I got the extra benefit of a hug. A real one. None of that self-conscious, hyper-straight-man shoulder-clapping business. Our torsos touched completely. Though the boat was grounded, it leaned slightly, (or maybe I was a bit off-balance), but it resulted in a slight rub at the groin. Shahid didn't flinch and kept his smile. For me it was as if lightning had struck and rewired my brain. It was as if my preference for the thirty-plus crowd, which suddenly seemed clinical, fell overboard. Several principles may have gotten kicked over as well. Mahmood stood stone-faced. I threw him a wink and a grin over Shahid's shoulder and mouthed the words *he's hot*. My right hand must have reached lower down Shahid's spine than usual in the ordinary "straight" forward embrace, because Mahmood's eyes followed with a scowl. I blew him a kiss. He's easy to tease, and it was a naughty moment I couldn't resist. The tension would work to our benefit tomorrow. Sex is always spicier on an edge.

Mahmood sat with us on the deck listening patiently to catch-up conversation and soon found he was a third wheel. He made a move to leave, and Shahid didn't insist that he stay longer, which surprised me. I asked Mahmood what time he'd come to get me next morning. As quickly as he said nine, Shahid said ten, which delighted me as much as it must have annoyed Mahmood. Bidding him a safe ride home, I shook hands with a grin and my thumb folded into my palm, which made him withdraw his hand as if he'd stuck his finger in a live electrical socket. He and Shahid exchanged puzzled glances while I feigned ignorance, and Mahmood turned and told me to have a good night, and then, with a sideward step so that Shahid couldn't see or hear, whispered *pig*. Yup, he and I were going to be hot tomorrow.

~

Just like the first time, I was the boat's only guest. We went out on the lake, returned as the sun was setting, and had the dinner his mother had prepared for us: simple but good chow, and it was veg, which I appreciated. She and Shahid's remaining unmarried sister had already retreated to their neighbour's boat, which they do whenever they host male guests. The electricity had gone out earlier in the day, and the boat's backup system was broken, so Shahid lit the table with candles. He looked positively studly, bigger in the amber glow that flickered over his full features, each one an asset: tan skin, thick jet-black hair, a generously sized but handsome nose, heavy lips, and the languid, liquid puppy eyes that said pet me, please. I was melting. I'd have him for dessert and lick my fingers afterwards. I was game, if he was willing.

I told him he'd changed a lot since the first time. He wanted to know how.

'You became a man,' I said.

'I became a man when I was twelve, when my father died.'

That wasn't how I wanted this to proceed. I vacillated. 'I know that. But you got grown-up looking. You put on muscle and now you can grow a beard.' And then stepping into a potential minefield, I tried to sound casual. 'And you have more than a bit of hair on your chest. Unusual for a guy your age.' I itched to run my fingers through the black tufts that rose above the second open button of his collared shirt.

'I got hairy early.'

His reply came across to me as terse, remote. I shrank. Could Shahid have thought that I found fault with his body? No, that would have been too easy. It wasn't that. In paying such close attention to his looks as I did, I calculated that I'd overstepped and crossed a line. A few moments of silence passed between us and then he rose and smiled. He seemed to have shaken off any issues. He proposed we move outside because the moon was up and with a cloudless sky there would be stars too. We moved back to the rear deck and onto the threadbare sofa that faced the water. We sat side by side, with legs touching. What had played out between us moments before didn't now mean that we had to keep space between skin. I was grateful for that.

I didn't know if I was back in the game, or if there ever was one with Shahid.

He repositioned himself and placed a friendly forearm on my shoulder, and at that moment I caught his scent. He was ripe after a day's work. I think it mad that foreigners dislike how our Indian men smell. For me the musk of crystallized sweat on a man is pure sex, and a direct connection to my dick. Though I've tried, I could never quite get myself to exude it, even when I don't use deodorant (weekends and holidays). My thoughts wandered to a not-so-distant memory. I've allowed myself the thrill of getting fondled twice on the Delhi metro, but it was the second experience that will forever sear itself in my memory. I got on a packed train at Rajiv Chowk, nudged my way into the crush, and squeezed in behind a guy with a glorious pong. We stood, his ass to my balls. He didn't shift. A sure sign. I inhaled. My cock leapt and swelled. He felt it. He turned carefully, and looking ahead into the crowd as if I didn't exist, ran his hand over my bulge, found the path of my erection (several degrees left of centre), and began an ever-so-discreet massage. He wasn't attractive, I never would have taken him home, but his pungent bouquet rendered that immaterial. The danger of having public sex in the middle of an unknowing mass of people heightened the moment, and though I'm not known for coming quickly in bedroom sex, a few strokes more and my stranger made me blow in my underwear. I had been holding my breath and exhaled long and slow. Staring ahead at the far end of the cars he never looked at me directly – but he smiled. He knew what he'd done. I got off at the next station, with my shoulder bag repositioned in front.

Sitting with Shahid's arm on my shoulder and catching whiffs of his musk, I thought I'd swoon. I hungered for him, but I needed a clearer signal, a green light. I've never been one to make the first move, especially toward a guy I'm not 100 per cent sure is gay. I can't cope with rejection. In the old days when I went to bars and clubs, I'd stake out a strategic spot, nurse a drink, scope out the crowd, give the one I liked the look, and wait for him to come to me. I met with success more often than not. At 48 I could still reel them in. I was fit, younger-looking than my age (so they said), and could fuck for hours. But these days hooking up online is easier. No getting ready to go out, no travelling, and no posing. An hour after the opening line he's at the door. But still, I never search and only answer messages from others. My reticence at moving first never worked against me thankfully, and I've managed to suck kilometres of handsome cock from one end of India to the other.

~

But with Shahid I was in unfamiliar territory. Even if he was interested, and that was far from certain, I was sure he wouldn't move first. I was his guest, and the Islamic code of hospitality, though indulgent, bears a formality that bars certain interactions between host and guest. Sex for one. But since I started thinking for myself in my early teens, cultural and societal barriers stood to be jumped. My challenge was to find a way to get Shahid on board, but for him to come to me. The hug and rub we started with earlier in the day was sexy enough, but his scent was now filling my lungs as we sat together, and lust and desire were in my blood.

At his side and knowing he was now legal to fantasize over, I wondered what he did with all the testosterone twenty-year-olds are famous for, while thinking that he wasn't allowed to use his dick for anything beyond pissing until he got married. Knowing too that young men don't always behave as they're commanded, my roving imagination led me into fantasizing how he might be dicking on the sly. It was inconceivable to me that a guy that divine, in his sexual prime, would be using his piece only to piss. I began to fixate on what it looked like: shape, size, and colour. That he was cut was certain. Did it curve upwards, to one side, downwards like a hook, or was it as straight as an arrow? Did it have a mushroom head or was it more like a plum? Was it thicker somewhere along the shaft or at the base? How would it smell and taste, if I could get my mouth on it? Don't young and horny guys just want their dicks sucked, with who's doing it a minor point of concern? My own cock began to stir. I stealthily stole a glimpse at his zipper. Not exactly the bulge I had hoped for, but there was a definite knob pushing through his jeans, which is more than most guys are able to show when you sneak a glance, hoping for a big surprise, and then wonder, disillusioned, where it could possibly be. I lost myself in my meanderings. Shahid had to have caught me checking him out.

~

My phone rang. Mahmood's name was blinking. I excused myself and took the call inside.

'How's it going? Having fun with the baby?'

I was defensive. 'He's good company. He can talk about more things than before. He's *mature*. We went out on the lake and now we're hanging out in the back. But no, I'm not having fun. Not yet. Very soon.'

Mahmood was taken aback. 'So you *are* trying to get him into bed.' There was a hint of scorn in his voice. 'You want him.'

'Let me put it this way, honey love. I'd eat his ass, swallow his dick, and drink his piss if he asked me.'

'You're depraved.'

'You'll see how much tomorrow,' I taunted. 'But don't worry about tonight. He was talking to me about the girls at his college when we were out on the lake. I'm sure he's not gay.'

'But curious,' he countered.

'Maybe. I don't know. I'll do my best recruiting.'

'Dirty dog.'

'Woof. Now put your dick back in your pants and stop masturbating over me. Behave, and tomorrow you get the real deal.'

'Bloody fool. You wish. Have fun.' I thought he'd hung up. But no, he'd only hesitated. 'And bring me a good story.'

~

I wanted a story, badly since the meditation on his cock. But the affection Shahid and I were sharing could well have been understood by him as the simple camaraderie between mates which Kashmiri men are known for. But the twist here was that he knew that I liked guys.

As a teenager I fell madly for an 'older' man of 27, a traveling German who let me hang out with him for a weekend. He was my first love, or so I'd imagined, though there was nothing physical between us except an honest embrace when we parted. Dishonest, but sexy embraces didn't start until a few years later at college. Fast-forward three decades and I wouldn't be able to guess how many men I've been in and out with since bachelor number one. Though an old hand at the game of seduction, I felt like I was driving without a steering wheel now. With Shahid I didn't know what to do.

I sank back into the sofa with him. The moon and stars shot streaks of light across the water. Few pictures were sexier than this. I closed my eyes and drifted. I saw Shahid place his left hand on my right knee, over which I placed my right hand. Our hands clasped instinctively. I saw myself rest my chin on his shoulder, breathe deep, and lightly brush my mustache across his cheek. I saw him turn slowly until his parted lips met mine. The tips of our tongues met. There we stayed, in the slightest of slow-motion movements, measurable in millimeters. I brought my left hand up to his shirt buttons, undid them, slid my hand in, and reached for the luxuriant black chest hair. I brought my lips to his neck, which he extended as I kissed and nibbled, collar to ear. He let out a resonant sigh that seemed to come from both of us.

I saw myself letting my hand fall into his lap. He was hard. I saw Shahid rise, grab my hand and lead me to my room. I don't know how the clothes came off. The video running in my mind skipped that scene. We were naked and he was on top of me. He put his tongue into my gaping mouth, grabbed a nipple with a fist, and slid his cock between my thighs and under my balls. I licked his neck with a wet tongue, pulled at his chest hair with my lips, and buried my face in the pit of his arm. I inhaled his sweaty musk. He pressed me into the bed, straddled me, placed his dick to my lips, pushed down to the balls, and face fucked me. I licked and sucked as if I were tasting cock for the last time. He sat on my face and I lapped the hairy crack of his butt like a dog in heat. He rocked back and forth and his dick slapped against my face. His sweat and my saliva ran down my cheek. I was slobbering like a madman. He repositioned himself, lifted my legs, licked his middle finger and put the tip in my ass. I was bucking like a horse. He held me down, and joined his tongue to his finger. I caught my breath and told him to wait. On went the rubber and lube.

I saw Shahid mount me and dive in. I turned my head to one side and groaned. Unlike the wild stabbing of many novices, his pace was slow and steady. Twenty years old and he was a pro. Within half an hour of his rhythmic fucking I was exhausted. I grabbed his hips and pulled him into me. He picked up the pace and I licked my hand to whack my dick, which he never touched. I like mutuality, but that didn't matter tonight. Shahid was a volcano. I serviced him with joy.

~

I slowly opened my eyes as if emerging from hypnosis.

'Everything ok with Mahmood?' Shahid asked, awakening me from my trance.

I took a breath and leapt, not knowing where I'd land.

'Mahmood's jealous.'

'Of what?'

'Of you. He thinks I want to sleep with you?'

'Do you?'

I felt a rush of adrenaline and my heart skipped a beat. I stammered. And then I remembered who I was. 'No. I don't. You're a great-looking guy, smart and sexy too, but you're my friend and I guess you're not gay, and even if you were, you're young enough to be my son. It would never work.'

He laughed. 'Thanks for saying those good things about me. I'm not gay, but we can still be friends, right? And I can say that you look nice too, right? You know, for your age. The guys must love you in Delhi.'

I smiled. 'Some do, maybe. I'm not sure.'

'Well I always liked you,' he continued. 'You were so nice to me when we went to Gulmarg three years ago. You bought me a ticket for the cable car without even asking me. No other guest ever did that before. They always leave me at the bottom. Remember when we were walking in those mountains and you were taking all those pictures of me. They're in a drawer in my room. I still have them.'

I didn't know what to say. My heart was stuck in my throat. At that moment I wanted to take him around the world. 'Next time I come we'll go again, or maybe to Pahalgam, or even Leh.'

Shahid was beaming. 'After I get my youngest sister married it will be my turn. You *have* to come to my wedding.'

'I will if you come to mine.'

He looked at me in amazement. 'You're getting married? I always asked you!'

I smiled. 'Maybe someday I will. But if and when I do, it will be to a man.'

We fell over ourselves laughing. He took my hand, shook it, and put his open palm over his heart. 'I'll come!'

Perfume

D'Lo

Sometimes I smell her perfume from across the street where she
Or someone who looks like her
   Is walking.

~

Seven months ago, I was 27. She was 34. I wonder if I'm going to walk with an air of all-knowing wisdom when I reach that age.

As part of an exchange programme, I had come to this place right at the northern edge of Vishakapatnam (or Vizag, the short 'cool kid' way to say it) to teach digital music recording. The management provided boarding for the teachers as well. We lived in the apartment complex next to the school. Our apartment had two rooms, with two teachers in each room. Both the computer teachers, Ms Neelu and Ms Vimal shared one room, while Ms Lakshmi and I shared the other. I think the management thought it would be more awkward to have me room in the men's quarters and therefore just stuck me with the women . . . in the room with

Ms Lakshmi. A square room with white square tiles holding up more than just the rectangle shapes of our low-to-the-ground full-size beds, the two box-like dressers and the small desk of thin sheet wood in the corner. This room held me together.

Ms Lakshmi (or Lux, as I called her because that was the nickname given to a cousin of mine) taught the children in the school how to read and, on her day off, she taught any woman in the area how to read.

But she did a lot more than teach reading. Anything. She did. She did anything. So yes, she worked for the people, she did.

Our beds were across from and diagonal to each other. Sometimes we'd sit up in our beds, facing each other from the opposite sides of the room. We'd talk. She told me that Ms Vijaya didn't approve of how she taught children, and was rigidly opposed to being tender with pupils, regardless of age. She told me about the chai wallah and how he keeps hitting on her even after she slapped him for squeezing her left breast. She shared with me how she was dropped off at a temple when she was a baby, was brought up by one of the priests and his sister and how, even though they have passed on, she still loved going back to her village because it was so green compared to this part of Vizag. She'd ask me about how things worked in the States, ask how my family took that I was queer, ask questions that veered dangerously close to the other questions she desired to ask, but she always pulled back in time. Eventually, without questions answered, but by watching me daily, observing me, she understood my masculinity. We could talk until the cocks crowed, right at 4:23 a.m., and worry about how hot the day would get and how much coffee it'd take to handle a full schedule, full classes and the electricity for the air con. going out at noon. But we talked more, and more, to let the fears dissipate, and when our whispers had to get quieter as everyone else in the house started taking their morning showers, she'd ask me to pull up the plastic purple stool, scoot nearer to her bed and we'd continue.

I'd see her on lunch breaks along with everyone else. She loved watching me interact with the other teachers; she said that only someone like me could be so bold and talk about taboo subjects with humour and ease. Someone like me – the American queer on Indian soil. She and I were the ones Ms Vijaya looked at out the corner of her eye, but we were also the ones that every young teacher craved to be around, to share their daily disgusts and triumphs with. Ms Lakshmi was like my wingman in that; without her being 'cool by me,' I wouldn't have had the perfect climate for everyone else to also accept me. My freak fetish factor was low in India.

~

Sometimes her smell preceded her, when she got home right before the sticky heat turned into cool sunset. She'd beg me to hit the rooftop with her. This part of the night was hers even before I came into the picture, and she would go without me easily, if I chose to stay put. But who would be that daft, to deny themselves her company
in those unfamiliar magical nights
they were for me

as she was
And what magic she made them more.

I recall, months later, how even walking up the spiral stairs outside the apartment building was done in quiet, and yet my heart pounded louder than our feet on the steel steps. I'd feel the thuds in my throat, an excitement for that alone time with her. The force of those heartbeats aiding me in getting up the stairs, while my Batas did me a disservice, feeling like flats of magnets.

I remember us lit like actors on set, but it was just that this village never slept.

It seemed like it could never get dark enough, so I hid my feelings within myself.

She watched me most at this time and shared deep, as our bottle of arrack became empty.

I could understand how it was easy for her to talk to me

I wasn't special, I was foreign

And she assumed that my homeland allowed me to be open to her secrets.

She had none, really.

Well, none that I would call secrets.

She might've fallen in love before, made passionate love and gotten her heart broken badly, she might've stabbed a man for attempting to rape her best friend, she might've walked and talked more brashly than Vizag would've liked. The shock factor was lower to someone like me – an American Transgender Queer.

To me, she was the big-hearted fish in a sea of hustling guppies and her swimming children were where she deposited her desires. She hoped they would sleep peacefully, in this village that never slept and she hoped that they would dream fantastically, the world beyond their village.

~

Sometimes, if we had a full bottle to start the night with, she sat on the low ledge of the balcony and would two-puff a beedi.

A simple pleasure for a *seemingly* simple woman.

She reclined with her complex thoughts and didn't mind when I –

What are you thinking, ma?

Oh, nothing. Just that times are changing.

The western world has poked his head out here enough and in different places.

The village sees a little, but wants it all –

and doesn't even know the extent of modernity.

and they don't know the price.

Yet, the desire is large enough to mask the downfall

and this is yet another British Imperialism done American but psychologically.

The question remains,

how do I get my people to think for themselves and not with the mob?

How do I show them the side that is not in neon offerings.

I resign.

I can only infiltrate their minds through their children's desires.

and I can only plant in the children, the desire to think.

I remember thinking to tell her that I said her very same words in America.

That I, too, wanted my village to think.

Sometimes I think back to the buildings with planes stuck in them. I remember hasty threats. Ignorance in Bed Stuy, in Park Slope, in every place I biked to get away from it. Sometimes I wonder why the world has forgotten American children. And I wonder, when American Powers die of old age, if their white children will be apt to carry on hatred, or if the children I teach, brown, black, yellow and white, will desire to be loved whole, so that hatred doesn't have a chance in the hundreds of growing bodies as they become who they need to be.

~

I remember looking at her and feeling her exhaustion as mine, but the streets had shown her how to have boundaries – she still burned bright and I remembered that burning out is what brought me there.

She loved her work, her people, herself. She didn't see any hope in it all, but she didn't need to. She saw potential through her faith, and that's the fuel she chose to run off of.

Sometimes she would begin to nod off on the ledge and I would tell her that she was scaring me; that she would fall accidentally. She would laugh and say that she was meant to go that way then, or that it would be just as well, to kill her rampant thoughts.

I remember her saying that if she fell, nothing would be missed. She knew damn well that everything in a ten-kilometre radius would be affected, or if not, fall to pieces.

She was not a fixture to me, not the horrendous painting in the hallway, the one of abstract flowers in pastels that no one paid attention to. She was the kettle I used to make tea for a relaxed morning of meditation and mindfulness. I needed her there, to forewarn me of the ways of this homeland of my ancestry. I needed her there, outside a homeland not secure for me. I needed her to keep me from running. From the paranoia of getting jumped from behind, from remembering the sound my left incisor made when it popped out as my face hit the concrete. The nurses over me saying, 'He's in a comatic state' and hearing the doctors refer to me as a girl. I needed a calm place while I sorted through the nights I don't remember when I barely made it home, after drinking deuce after deuce, knocking on friends' doors or sleeping outside of them. I needed to stop and breathe and remember how my loved ones, the ones I chose as family, saw their own pain in my self-hatred. I needed her and India to remind me what strength is.

Sometimes, after the local brew and roll-up cigs could be passed no more, I would scoop her droopy body up in my arms, and while she protested against being carried, she never did it with much resistance.

I wanted to be the one to carry her revolutionary thoughts. And if I could, I wanted to lift her up above the chaos and set her on the platform to share in all the things she loved.

~

I remember that one night, after carrying her and settling her in her bed, I asked if she wanted to change out of her sari. She always made a sound that said she couldn't be bothered but then always pointed to her pins in her sari's pleats. I undid them, as I had done many times before . . . That particular night, she touched my wrists sweetly and sleepily.

~

The next night, we were in our own play. We made small talk to kill time. I waited for her to feign sleep, she waited for me to scoop her up off the ledge. She waited for me to ask her if she needed me to loosen up her sari, and I almost didn't wait until she pointed to her pins. That night, however, I struggled for a minute or two and finally when undone, I looked to see if I had awakened her from her half-sleep. She was looking at me with fully-open brown eyes.

I became terrified, but instinctively knew to appease the tension by covering her up, turning to shut off the light, and slipping into my bed.

Sometimes it took me a long time to fall asleep.

The next morning, thankfully a weekend morning, I tiredly woke up to the kettle whistling. She, fresh out the bath with damp hair, boiled water for both my tea and her coffee. She must've been struggling with sleep too, because while all else was in silver steel glasses, she reached for the ceramic mug from Ohio and it came crashing down. The cracked handle cut her ever so lightly on the top of her foot. She cursed a 'shit' and hopped to the chair to examine her injury.

I offered my assistance and knelt to help diagnose the next action to be taken for the wound. She kicked me with her good foot. I told her I wasn't going to hurt her, went to the bathroom and returned with alcohol and a band-aid. I had already seen that the cut was small, yet the kick I received to my shoulder would have to be nursed further. After losing both my patience and kindness, to my own surprise, I sternly and American-ly told her to 'calm the fuck down' and didn't mind that I cursed at her, about her, to her for the first time. I guess I hadn't fully dissipated the tension from last night.

~

She sat quietly. I cleaned her wound, anticipating a scream or some violent reaction to the alcohol swab. I braced for another kick. Instead, she grabbed her calf as if to stop the pain from shooting up her leg. I continued cleaning the area around the wound and looked up. Her forehead had sweat. To balance both of us out, I picked up her leg and steadied it on my knee to place the band-aid. And this final action was my death to thinking clearly any further.

I smelled her, through the pleats and the cotton folds of her sari as the shift in her seat sent air through her legs. I nearly turned beast. I wanted to stay there, even after my trance-like placement of the band-aid. I wanted to stay kneeling in front of her spread, lightheaded with a scent that triggered pleasure-filled emotions.

I took her hand from her calf, replaced it with mine and a massage, pulling her sari back to safety, over her legs while rethinking the action. My heart would not let me behave human. It pulsed the desire of an animal in heat and I instinctively kissed her knee, disguising it as giving blessings for a quick recovery when all I really wanted to do was pull her into me and inhale deeply the aroma through her sari. And so I did.

Sometimes I wonder if she knew at that instant.

If she'd wanted to allow herself, she could've slapped me at the sight of my head inhaling between her legs. She didn't. Though I remember, seconds before, she was about to turn the tension switch to off: make light of her silly reaction to a small cut. She was about to get up off the chair and continue making tea and coffee. She grabbed my head to say thankyou.

I was already taken by another spirit.
I wasn't afraid of looking at her now.
And now, she knew.

We stared at each other. I saw her smile turn to fear. My hand rose up to hold her wrist, while her palm still held my head. And I kissed that place, the inside of a delicate wrist, those two veins touched both my lips, I kissed her wrist.

~

She was still. Still. Stiff. Waiting like a deer knowing his death as I lifted her sari just up past her knees and kissed both caps. Kissing them as if they were the lips that kept me awake every night while I kissed them in my mind. I pulled her sari further up to the top of her legs, put my face against the skin of her lap, before pulling the sari back over me; pulling the sari over the kisses I placed on the inside of her thighs, pulling the sari back over to cover the desire that was turning me into this lion-like animal.

It didn't matter I was covered. She knew what possible

damage for our future I was doing with my kisses under her sari. Both thighs, insides.

And then as if I was the only one who could stop the train, I stopped and stayed there. Inhaling. Buried under the sari.

~

I stayed there, kissing her thighs while the seconds oozed to another measure of time . . . a sort of long second that made long minutes. Her scent getting stronger with each kiss. The vapours I let seep into my nose, down my throat, filling up each lung slowly with fruit and flower, peach-coloured vapours.

And just as I was to flick my tongue closer to the crevice of hair meets soft inner thigh, she slowly pulled the sari from over my head. Was she trying to shame me? Or engage me? Reality could be so damn harsh with this much blood pumping in my body. I didn't raise my head in case.

A tear hit the back of my neck. I touched it and tasted it. Got up and slowly kissed the salt trails from off her face. Faces close, I moved in gently and kissed her lips. Finally. And softly, first – to see the reaction on her face – to the fact that the steam off my face smelled of that familiar place on her body and that familiar smell was on a foreigner's face.

Allowing my desire to shift out of my way, I saw the face of a warrior leaking streams hesitantly. She kissed me back, at first to reciprocate, soft and moist and salty. She kissed me to say it was ok and right.

And then . . . she got lost. Her lips showed hunger. Deep, passionate, our lips fit perfectly around and on each other. And boy, could this one kiss. She kissed my past days of yearning for her. She kissed her days of feeling lonely here. She kissed all the tension, these kisses of gratitude. And she kissed my childhood, my face with a popped-out tooth. She kissed me like band-aids. And only after that kind of kissing healed every wound, did we kiss differently. We kissed and kissed and kissed.

More kisses released from her past came flooding out of her being. And just as we were losing grips and balance, she wrapped her limbs around me, pulled me deep and strong to her, and I picked her up like I had done many times before, but this time like a child, not the wife I walked over doorframes with. We kissed all the way back to the room which held our beds. We told the room that it didn't need to hold our tension anymore.

Landing gently on her bed, we slowly began to make love, letting time get enveloped in the creases of the linens.

~

My lips to her neckside, travelling to both sides, inhaling the sandalwood soap still on her skin, letting her wet wisps of hair kiss me back. I unbuttoned her blouse at the top, letting her breasts rise up from her soil to greet the sun from my eyes. And my lips kissed while her body rose to meet them. Out of the pain of waiting, one of her hands unbuttoned the rest of her blouse and she reached for her left breast with one hand, and shoved my head towards it with the other. She didn't let go of my head until I had her nipple in my mouth and kicked it around with my tongue. By the sounds she made, I could tell she was holding back. Holding her breast up and out for me to suck and lick and kiss, she wriggled under me – and when she had enough, the other breast was on standby as she shoved my head in that direction. And as soon as I had the other nipple properly between my lip-covered teeth, pressing down with just enough pressure, immediately pouring out of her lips came a deep sigh of relief, of pleasure, all of which made the heat in my boxers unbearable. With both my hands on her bare breasts, and my lips taking turns on them, she moved ever so slightly under me, allowing her mound to press up against my leg. I knew she was getting close, so I quickly pulled my hands off her and turned her to her side. She protested, but I pressed up against her firmly from behind. I had waited too long for this to not to last for a long time.

I kissed the back of her neck, tickling her with the heat from my mouth, my patches of stubble and my tongue. She squirmed as far away as my grip would allow her, but never too far to come back for more. After minutes of anguish, she desperately tried to take charge. I knew if I reached around and touched her in between her legs, she would have gotten what her body wanted right away. Again, I had waited too long for this moment.

So I slipped off the bed with my knees on the ground, adjusting her body towards me. Once her waist was in my hands, I slid her towards me by placing her legs over my shoulders. She tried to shove my head right into her, but I wouldn't have it. I licked the sides of her mound, slowly and cautiously, careful not to enter her yet, enjoying every molecule that escaped from inside of her. I wanted every last drop in my mouth and not lost in her sari, on the bed or on the floor. My restraining her was confusing her, but she was not going to spoil the moment I didn't even know I was preparing for. After all, this might be a one-time shot.

After a while of her moaning out the names of her gods, I decided to stop. She dug her hands into my shoulder as if to slap me for being so cruel. Forcing her to stand, I stepped her over to the wall nearest the bed and kissed her passionately, letting her lick my face, coated with her scent. Her breasts were pressed up against my flat chest, and though my newly-grafted nipples were de-sensitized, my whole chest was on fire. I wanted to press up against her harder, I just needed to feel that close, that smashed-up on someone, to almost become one. I continued to touch her on my way down to the floor, squeezing and teasing just to hear more of these new sounds I never knew about.

Once on the ground, I lifted all the sari pleats and skirt to her waist, placed my mouth on her dripping clit and licked her juices, still without entering her. I knew she would make me more. And how she did. It seemed like she wasn't going to stop. Her juices were running down the inside of her leg, and I followed the stream upwards towards her door and finally entered. My tongue was in as far as it could go and she rode it. Her body slowly going up and down, my nose rubbing against her clit. These were different sounds. We stayed like this for a lifetime, losing grip on the baggage we were tired of holding onto so tight. And then, all of a sudden, she grabbed me by the shoulders and lifted me off the ground with such ferocity. She told me that she couldn't take it anymore and whispered, 'Please, Mr Jay, can you please?'

I guess it was the earnestness in her tone, the fact that she and I had embarked on a journey we knew we'd have to process at a later time, or that neither one of us had had sex in a long time. I listened to her.

We moved back to the bed and I rubbed her whole body as she lay in front of me. I rubbed her as if I was giving an ayurvedic massage, pushing upwards from her belly, over her heart and out above her shoulders. And when I could sense she was calm, I went down between her legs, pulled up her sari and continued again. First in circles and figure eights around her clit, over and over with an increase of tempo, and right when her temperature rose again, I entered her with my two fingers. She started wailing a song with each thrust in and out and in between. I steadied my pressure with my tongue and let my fingers pull upwards, *just a little*, to hit her special spot. In between her moans, in the milliseconds of quiet calm, you could hear the sounds of lapping and of my finger in her volcano of liquid fire, and with every shift in my body to greet hers, you could faintly hear a similar sound coming from inside my jeans; a beautiful re-mix of her body and mine stirring together our bodies' liquid desires.

We were in motion, on this ocean.
We moved in sync and my tongue did tricks.
Her pelvis shifted down, I pulled up more.
She rode my fingers, and rode my tongue.
Her body bucked and danced against both points of pleasure.

And right as she came, her hands reached out and grabbed my head. I saw her stomach clench upwards and she quaked under me, hard; the loudness of her screams muffled by her thighs suffocating me. I felt her clit pulse in my mouth, and her insides constrict my fingers like a ring she was putting on me to ensure I would stay committed in her. She quaked some more until it had all left her body, until the ring left my fingers, until her clit landed like a marble back in a groove. And when she was finally relaxed and released, after the last aftershock, I looked at her. She was glorious. Spent, but glowing. Smiling and crying. We held each other until she slept.

I also fell asleep, but woke to her hands in my pants, and her mouth on mine, kissing me again. I told her I wasn't ready that morning; that eventually I might be, but that I needed some time. I told her that it's harder to release my grip from my baggage around my body. She responded with, 'That's why you came here, to go back home empty-handed and lighthearted.'

~

Seven months later, and every day since, I wake up with her head in my neckside. And almost three to four times a week, I wake up with her hopeful hands in my boxers. Today might be the day she smells me.

Jewel and the Boy

Abeer Hoque

SPRING

1.

The closet is hot and dark and something sharp is pressing into his calf. Still Jewel pulls him close, closer. The boy is hesitating, he can tell, not outwards, but in that inside way that makes bodies heavy. Jewel knows that hesitation too well. He feels it himself even now, but he has never been able to stop himself when it comes to touching. Once when he was a baby, he had battered a lit candle. The wax had slipped slow motion, hardening on his hands. Even as he was hauled off screaming, his mother said he had been reaching still, looking still.

His hands are holding the boy's torso, ribs sharp, muscles smooth, arms by his own sides. Jewel moves his hands to his chest and slides them on up, past collarbones, funnelling his throat, the boy's face a flower in his palms. The boy's hips give a little, lean for a tender second against Jewel, and he feels the light shoot from the base of his spine, down down.

2.

Jewel sees the boy on Bancroft. He thinks to turn away, but Jewel shakes his head smiling.

'Walk with me,' he says, almost touching the boy and then not. 'I don't bite.'

South on Hillegass, and after Derby, a park spreads itself out and down. In the corner near the toilets that no one except the homeless people use is where Jewel takes his shoulder. The boy turns, and his mouth catches up so quickly that Jewel knows he was waiting for it, hoping for it.

'Do you know why?' Jewel asks when he lets up. They are holding hands on one side, the other side free.

'Because I want it,' the boy says in his honeyed voice. Everything about him is honey, his skin, his hair, his eyes, his Bengali accent blended into Berkeley cool. When Jewel scrunches his eyes, the boy himself is a molten blur.

Jewel laughs. He knows it takes a pair to say it like that, the other way round. To say it out loud. To make it real.

3.

When Jewel kisses the boy, he knows it's the right thing. In the now, here, this world anyway. The boy's tongue is like air on silver. Jewel feels it oxidising him, turning him into someone else. Someone who wants. Someone who feels. He straightens, lifts the boy's arms, presses his wrists to the wall. The boy's head jerks forward, their mouths colliding. He has all the time in the world. He can kiss him all night and the age after.

'Fuck,' the boy whispers. 'Fuck.'

Jewel pulls him in, hand splayed on the back of his head. He imagines the light trying to find a way between their bodies, failing. The boy holds on to him like he's drowning. Jewel is torn between hating the boy for his submission and wanting nothing less.

'Is this what you wanted?' the boy says, his voice hoarse, clever, clear.

The question slaps Jewel back to attention.

4.

The boy is standing close, too close. Jewel feels the charge building. Soon, the space between their hands will be nothing more than a live wire. Before this can happen, the boy jumps ahead. His pinky hooks with Jewel's and Jewel's heart jumps into his mouth. It's dangerous, this touching in such a public place, surrounded by everyone who cannot know what's happening behind Jewel's back. His face is burning, but he cannot, will not, pull his hand away.

His thumb starts on the inside of the boy's wrist. It slides up to the centre of his palm and pushes into the soft hot, his other four fingers splayed on the back of the boy's hand. He holds his hand in this way, in a way the boy cannot hold back, can only be held, in a way that says you're mine, not I'm yours.

SUMMER

5.

When the boy dances, there's nothing Jewel likes better than to watch him. He looks like one of those temple statues on Russell Street, arms rigid and liquid at the same time, feet deliberate precise light. Trance playing on the boom.

'You were such a fag,' Jewel says inhaling that first sweet drag.

The boy stands still, his eyes sideways watching Jewel.

'Such a beautiful fag.'

'There were no daughters in my family,' the boy says, 'much to my mother's grief. So I had to do the needful. I had to learn how to dance.'

Jewel feels caught in his gaze, like he can't go anywhere, not even behind him, without those eyes following. He puts down his smoke, stands up, tries to follow the molasses motion. The boy's arms come around him, cup his elbows, hip checked, his hands lingering. Jewel feels himself fitting into the pose, the pose fitting to him, a bodily click.

'Stay,' he says to Jewel, walking away.

Now Jewel follows him with his eyes. Willingly, he thinks.

6.

Jewel is listening to the boy tell him a story. In the story, Jewel blindfolds the boy. So Jewel blindfolds the boy. He uses the boy's scarf. It smells like incense.

'Patchouli? Sandalwood?' Jewel taunts.

'My mother gave it to me, before I left home. But maybe you don't want to know what happens next.'

'What happens next?'

'Next you fuck me,' the boy says.

Jewel kisses him, all mouth, no hands. His hands are putting on the condom.

'Then,' the boy says in between kisses, 'all your friends fuck me, one by one, while you watch.'

Jewel pauses and looks at him. He shakes his head, squeezes the tip of the condom briefly.

'You're harder than ever, aren't you?' the boy asks.

It's true. Jewel kisses him once more and enters.

7.

The boy is asleep in the chair, naked as the heated day. Jewel has no chance of carrying him to bed, so he stands by the chair and looks out the window. Darkening, and all he sees are the two of them against dirty glass. Twined and tired, the boy looks younger than ever, despite the years he has on Jewel. His head is against one arm, the other arm down the inside of his thigh, as if drawing a curtain.

The boy wakes up. In one slow move, like he is born to do this, he turns and languishes against Jewel. He stays like this, cheek against bare thigh, not taking him into his mouth, only breathing next to him, waiting. Fire breath, teeth bared, mouth shaped to swallow.

Jewel watches their reflection. He says, 'Vision of loveliness.'

'Would that it were more than that,' says the boy, making Jewel look down.

Before he can say anything, the boy shrugs and when his mouth makes contact, Jewel feels it like a loss.

8.

His hand always starts at the boy's face, the angular rise of his cheek, the eyelashes L'Oreal thick. He presses the flat of his hand against the square of his jaw, and waits for the boy to turn into his palm. When he does, he kisses him.

His hand always starts at the boy's cock, the baby soft foreskin, the spring hair. He encircles the base, palm flat, fingers hiding everything but the growing shaft. He waits until he can just see the head, dew ruby, egg in an egg cup. When he does, he kisses him.

Sometimes when Jewel touches the boy, he can't imagine anybody else. Not just touching anyone else, but he can't remember that anyone else exists. Even his own self dissolves and every memory he ever had goes along with it. It is only the touching that remains, out of body, out of time.

MONSOON

9.

The party howls outside. The boy is leaning against the bathroom sink facing Jewel, arms folded. Jewel takes his elbows and turns him around. The boy places his hands on the counter, straightens his elbows, looks in the mirror at Jewel. Jewel unbuttons the boy's jeans, pushes them on down. He isn't wearing anything underneath. He unbuckles his own belt and pulls the boy's hips back into himself hard. Skin to skin. Cock to ass. Hand to head, pushing down.

Someone bangs on the door, but Jewel is pulling away even before that. The boy's eyes narrow. Light bursts from his mouth.

'I don't want none but kisses,' Jewel says.

The boy turns around, pushes him against the wall. Jewel can see their reflections, hoar and sepia.

'I'll give you what you ask for,' the boy says kissing him, the light still emanating. Jewel swallows the shining, each kiss, fear disremembered.

'Even if it's not what you want.' The boy's mouth moves to his cock, wet on wet.

Jewel comes in a minute flat and pulls the boy up to kiss him. The banging has started again. How long have they been in the bathroom? A second? An hour? He kisses him again, and again.

'I want,' he says, come and the boy's sweet on his tongue, 'Nothing else were true.'

10.

The boy is angry. Jewel knows it. He also knows he can't say anything because it would only make things worse. Instead he picks on him. He leans across the boy's bare lap and gestures to the coffee table.

'Your shite were everywhere,' he says, 'You can't put nothing away.'

He knows the papers are for him, that the boy went looking for them. The boy pushes him off, as Jewel knows he will, and starts cleaning up.

Jewel leans back and away and flicks another flame, 'Did you call your mother?'

The boy stops for a split and then keeps going.

Finally, Jewel pulls the last straw and says, 'I gotta go.'

The boy fights with himself not to react, but when Jewel moves to stand, he does too. He takes Jewel's arm and then his throat, pushing him back down. The motion is fluid, automatic, as if ordained. So then the next thing that happens, must.

The boy is crying as he pushes at Jewel, between serrate kisses. Jewel is telling him not to. It's only the beginning, Jewel is saying, knowing it to be the truth.

'There is no beginning,' the boy says, his tears running into his wet mouth. Jewel licks the tears as they come. 'Only what comes after.'

'Then this were what come after,' Jewel says, putting his hand on the boy's heated body and then on his own. 'This.'

'This.'

11.

The boy wakes Jewel in the morning with a blowjob. The curtains are drawn, the sheets wrinkled and stale. He starts up slow, lips closed, just touching. Then he takes Jewel's cock into his mouth like butter won't melt. He rolls the head around in his mouth, presses it up down sideways with his tongue. When it starts to swell, he lets go, kisses off into the insides of his thighs. Jewel is still asleep, but now his dream is weighted and wet. When the boy takes him back into his mouth, he sucks harder, wider, tongue down the base, up the back seam, hooking under the hood. Jewel's dreaming is fizzed, ready to pop. He wakes up not sure if he's ready to piss himself or come. He wakes up knowing release is all that. Give it to a man, and the rest is in his hands. Gladly.

THE DRY SEASON

12.

The first time isn't like a firebrand up his ass. It's like a fire engine, and Jewel is the fire. The boy stops when he cries out.

'Don't stop now,' Jewel grits out.

'Are you sure?' The boy's thighs are taut. He moves to kiss the back of Jewel's neck and inadvertently pushes deeper.

Jewel closes his eyes. 'Yes.'

He's gripping the exposed piping along the edge of the mattress. The sheet has long since rolled off and is somewhere under his belly. The mattress label pasted onto the corner crackles under his arm, the sound as fragile as he feels. He will do this once. For the boy. So he can say he's done it. So he knows what it's like.

Even as the feeling flares and feints and flares again, he knows he's lying. He will do everything again. Even the things that hurt the most. Especially those.

13.

Jewel swishes his belt out of the loops. It leaves the bone curve of his hips, marks the air with the opposite sine, then falls by his side. He pulls the boy's wrists together, binds the belt around them, and then buckles it to the bedpost. The boy is helpless, liquid with laughter. Jewel's face is still, stern. He's playing his part even if the boy won't.

'Stop your laughing,' he hisses. 'You want a beating too?'

The boy's laughter dies away. 'Yes, please,' he says, 'With a cupped palm.'

'You don't get to choose how,' Jewel says flipping him over rough.

The boy cries out and Jewel turns him back quickly. His eyes are screwed shut, his mouth slightly open. Jewel leans down to kiss him in apology. In doing so, his hip brushes against the boy's cock. It's hard. He grins.

14.

Jewel rounds the bed in time to the music. Pastoral harp, over the top, perfect. The singer's voice is lazy, level, despite the hunger lyrics. The boy is sitting up, arms hugging his shins, chin on his knees. He licks his lips. It's what he does just before he kisses Jewel, even if he's only thinking about it.

Jewel laughs. 'I know what you're thinking.'

He leans in close enough to see the creases in the boy's dry lips, the faintest pock on his left cheek, lashes individual. The boy looks at him, chin still planted, hair falling in his eyes. He has a generous well-shaped mouth, lips dark and defined like they were painted on. He's beginning to smile. He almost licks his lips again but stops himself. Jewel thumbs his lower lip out. When he releases, the boy's mouth remains slightly open. Still he doesn't move. For the longest time, Jewel watches him, and for once, neither of them is waiting.

AUTUMN

15.

They are lying in the back of the car, the night violet and loamy. Jewel's arm is looped lazy around his head. The boy lies on him like an electric blanket, as they look up at the trees with their branches waving at the wind.

'My sweet,' Jewel whispers in his ear, 'nothing.'

The boy rolls his eyes smiling. A leaf slaps against the car, slicks down the side. Jewel slides his hands under the boy's trench, down his jeans. The boy judders at the cold but sucks in to let him in.

Jewel roams his hands down his thighs. Back up. Back on down. Back up again. Even when his palms finally warm, he stays clear of the centre, away from the heat. Instead he kisses the boy's neck, sucking, licking, biting. The boy arches, his arms trapped under Jewel's, his cock brushing past elusive hands, a fluke move, inflaming. Jewel keeps biting, licking, sucking.

'Please stop,' the boy says, turning to Jewel in fluent desperation, 'Please don't stop.'

Jewel nods. He covers the boy's mouth with his, lets him arch into his opening hands.

16.

The boy's head is on Jewel's stomach, looking down his legs. He can hear his stomach talking, feel his breath like a wave under muscle and skin. His hand lazily traces Jewel's thigh, elbow crooked around hipbone.

He turns his head up to look. Jewel is looking out the window, the one without a view, night or day. The blank light comes and keeps coming. It spreads over them, covers the bed, reaches for the warped wooden floor, fails. He looks back the other way, Jewel's navel at his lips.

'What do you want?' Jewel asks, running his hand through the boy's hair.

'Nothing,' the boy says. He can feel his heart. 'Nothing I don't have already in spades.'

17.

Jewel can feel the drip down his throat, the metallic tang, the coiling ready. The boy is dancing like the world is going to end, like it's his last chance. Jewel doesn't have time for pleasantries. It has to happen now. He pulls him out of orbit and into his own whirl. The boy resists. He doesn't want to fuck like the world is going to end. He wants to dance.

Jewel jerks and he twists and falls. Grace yet. He turns him to face him as the boy tries to recover. He doesn't want to fight. He just wants a transition. But Jewel's energy is monstrous, manic. It washes over the room like a wave, leaving only single-mindedness in its wake.

'Fuck,' the boy whispers as he struggles, 'Fuck, just stop, for one second. Listen to me.'

Everything is shards, slanting, harmful. The boy's voice is underwater, reaching Jewel as if after miles, years. Over that distance, the boy comes to see that the farther he goes, the more Jewel reaches out. So he knows what he must do, what he must keep doing.

'It's not that simple,' Jewel says.

The boy is frightened into stillness, as much by Jewel's scorn as the words.

'Nothing were ever that blood simple.'

WINTER

18.

When Jewel walks into the room, the boy is perched on the arm of the couch like a monkey. He pounces and Jewel play falls and then fall falls. The rug below them is thin enough to feel the floorboards underneath. The boy's hand reaches around, grabs his cock, and Jewel feels it like a glove, the last jigsaw piece. He's hard in seconds but the boy won't let him have his way with him. Instead he plays Jewel for a song.

Jewel sings, *This could go on forever . . . would that it would . . . would that it would . . .*

The boy is late blooming, holding him so close that Jewel is singing into his skin. He holds Jewel's face so their eyelashes touch. They make love like this, face to face so they can kiss. Jewel knows his taste like it's his own, except, joyously, not.

Each thrust and the boy comes closer and closer and closer. As he comes, tears come into his eyes, they leave.

Jewel keeps singing, *This could stop right now . . . would that it would . . . would that it would . . .*

19.

Jewel is sitting, the boy on his lap facing him, naked, wearing only a headlamp. The last light is blown, the only other light from the bathroom. Jewel is rolling a joint between them, the goods spread out on a plate beside them. He's using the rolling papers the boy got him.

'Who'd have thought?' he says, licking, rolling, laughing.

'Thought what?' the boy says looking up, the light sharping into Jewel's face.

Jewel squints, his irises shifting proportion, pigment. 'That you'd be lighting my way.'

The boy laughs and switches off the headlamp. He kisses him and Jewel puts the tray aside, kisses him back hard and hungry.

'I must go,' the boy says getting up, switching the headlamp back on, picking up his clothes.

'Must you?' says Jewel in mimicry.

'Godknows, I were so crying late,' the boy shoots back just as quick a mime.

Jewel smiles, his irises modulating again. 'Leave the light, yeah?'

The boy hesitates as he buttons his jeans.

'Or don't,' Jewel says in amusement, 'I'll finish in the bathroom.'

The boy throws his light at him and Jewel catches it like he knew it was coming all along. He knows to make up for the sass, so he doesn't start licking and rolling just yet. He watches the boy pull on his t-shirt, arms first, knowing he'll feel him watching. He watches him pocket his keys, open the door. And then just as he's closing the door, Jewel calls out his love.

20.

The boy cuts into a peach with Jewel's Swiss Army knife. Each new moon reveals a rust core, its skin curling loverly. He eats the peach standing over the sink, dripping, his hands cupped in prayer.

Jewel watches him from the doorway. He knows it's a gift, what he has. He wants to take the knife and cut them both, stop the picture of now, in this moment. Instead every second takes them farther, into the coming gloaming, the inconceivable morning. What he will remember of now will be some pale decay. Better to leave history unremembered, undamaged.

He walks over and with one hand, takes the knife, wipes it clean, switches it closed. With the same hand, his knife hand, he touches his knuckle to the boy's cheek. The silence following will hold this moment, will carry it to its grave, so no one else has to.

Give Her A Shot

Msbehave

PERSON 1

Plunging recklessly, it was deeper than last time. Exciting and scary at the same time ... it was the best time to look, while she was busy mixing a drink for me. I didn't want her to know what effect it had on me. Dangling precariously above her delicious swell, brushing it occasionally, was a golden charm. As she leaned over to hand me the highball glass, the charm rocked back and forth till it nestled into the alcove fashioned by breasts jostling against biceps. Warmth surged up me, a growing consternation – had she figured out that necklines have an effect on me? I was quite sure that I hadn't betrayed any emotion the last time – she had worn a red shirt and left one too many unbuttoned. Now, a décolletage framed by a deep and gauzy black 'V' – an escalation, a progression on her part. I tried to tell myself I was being paranoid. Maybe I had stared too long or maybe this was the second time I was focusing on her breasts. But, had she bent down too deep? Did she linger longer than she should have? Anything was possible. My fingers felt wet and sticky all of a sudden as I groped for a response to her, calling me back to earth.

I wiped off the condensation from my fingers. My other hand was damp from sweat. Was she as painfully aware of my own awkward movements as I was? This was the second time we were meeting after the drunken make-out at the drag party. I had no clue what she liked – the alcohol had left our initial encounters hazy. Couldn't even say whether she liked to take the initiative or preferred to sit back. What if she was one of those people who took umbrage at being read the wrong way? We were obviously meeting for sex, dammit; I had been hasty in saying yes to this date. Though the very sight of her sent quivers coursing through me – towering height, thundering hair and the lightning-sharp nose.

Tonight, she was storming my bastions, and I wasn't ready. What if cardinal mistakes were made and I left her dissatisfied? I began considering opening gambits. Maybe I could offer to help with the drinks in the cheek-by-jowl kitchen and skim a fingertip along her pronounced shoulder blades. Or would I look like the cheap guy in the theatre who snakes an arm around his date? I could sit next to her, clothes grazing and the gradual linger that would see flesh meeting flesh. Would that be too slow? We weren't out for a romantic dinner after all.

A few nervous gulps later, my glass was empty. She had started mixing the next round of drinks, ice rattling furiously as her hands went snap, jerk, up and down with the shaker. This would be a good time to approach her – that coiled, controlled power in her arms had given me a head rush. I could imagine that strength being used on me, arms encircling me or the firm pressure of her palms on my body. The L-shaped platform in the kitchen jutted out unkindly, trying something sexy would be awkward. Logistically, I wasn't clear on how or what could happen. I didn't want to fall flat on my face. The drink fizzed loudly as she topped it up with soda.

PERSON 2

I decide to sit down next to my date. Dipping neck-lines had worked for me in the past, but with her, not even a compliment. In fact, I wonder whether she had noticed at all, she was verging on the platonic tonight. Our initial meetings had seen us both drunk and tongue-loose in more ways than one. I was taken by a surprising attraction when I first saw her at the party. Plaid shorts, white shirt and suspenders and a Gatsby jauntily perched on her head. Her sexiness was casual and indifferent, like last night's clothes thrown over a chair. Just when I thought that my flirting had gone in vain, she asked me to join her for a smoke. I was led to a narrow, dark utility passage with criss-crossing ventilators and dropping wires, where she backed me into a corner and kissed me without preamble. As her tongue entered my mouth, I felt her thumbs press into the sides of my throat. As we leaned into each other, my overwhelming wetness pushed back against me.

We blew smoke out of a tiny cubby-hole of a window after we were done. The second time we met was at a grungy bar for drinks and dancing. Taking frequent turns to buy rounds of beer on a humid night, we ended up having a quickie in the women's bathroom. The metal latches clanged, basins ran water, flushes gurgled, and people borrowed make-up as we unzipped each other's pants. Four legs akimbo, thirsty kisses, furious fingers and groans silenced at the top of the throat. To top it all, the pleasure of sex amidst people who lived in homo-oblivion. Despite my drunkenness, thoughts of those kajal-rimmed eyes, black and white ceramic rings and the smell of her perfume found their way into my bed the night after our bar-bathroom sex. The gentle flicks of her thumb along my clit and the pendulous folds of her clit made me want unabashedly naked sex with her. To taste and see what I'd been touching.

Today, she didn't evince any sexual interest in me, despite my attempts at dress-up. The way she sprawled on my sofa, nonchalant and somewhat distant, made me so hot for her. In the privacy of my typically-Bombay one-room studio, I envisioned a finger running along the 'V' of my neckline. Or her leaning over the kitchen counter to give me a kiss. I pulled out my best bartender shake and hoped she would drink me in with those arresting eyes, but she was lost in her own thoughts. Her ample view of my breasts had only resulted in a blank look, forget the grasp, grope, squeeze and pull I was craving for. Her moist lips were barely responding to my conversation, forget sexual overtures. But my need for her body, her touch, our sex was fuelling a pushy and overt seduction as I lay a hand on her thigh soon after I sat down next to her. There was an immediate stiffening in her body followed by an uncomfortable silence in the air.

PERSON 1

I was having difficulty breathing and felt my chest was perceptibly heaving. Her hand sitting there solidly had made my hamstring tense up and it would be very embarrassing to get a cramp now. I wasn't quite sure what to do with myself, should I move? Stay still? I was probably supposed to do something. Her gaze was unflinching as her index finger traced the seam of my jeans. I couldn't bear to look down at those well-shaped fingers nor did I have the guts to look up at her face. Snatches of sensation came my way, nails digging into my shoulder as she stifled a moan, her hand sliding smoothly past my briefs – it felt really good. Tonight, those confident fingers and their assured touch were giving me the shivers right down to the soles of my feet.

I felt like resting my hand on top of hers so I could feel those pronounced knuckles sloping up into me. A kickboxing fan, she had balled her hands up and thrown a few fists at her punching bag and I had loved the resounding thwack of her knuckles on canvas. I wondered how those long legs would look as they snapped out in a kick. I could lace my fingers into hers and press into her thighs. Were her fingers apart far enough? Should I push them apart? Would she think that my hand in hers was a romantic gesture? I didn't want to kill the mood. It was too awkward to place my hand atop hers.

She was close enough for me to reach out and give her a light kiss on the lips. Feeling brave, I hunched forward slightly. She stayed where she was, not moving away nor near. Her hand stayed on my thigh. And, I froze. Now I was stuck, I should have just done it quick instead of building anticipation. It had become one of those awkward moments. After that pause, I couldn't kiss her briefly and pull back quickly. I knew it would lead to more – kissing, touching, feeling, stoking and stroking.

But I wasn't ready, it was much too soon, I couldn't imagine responding to her right now. When I said I needed more ice, she paused wordlessly and got up from the sofa. Watching the vast stride of those long legs – my tall woman fantasy was being fulfilled. Watching as she cracked the ice-tray into my drink – appreciating her from a distance was so much easier than dealing with her brimming sexuality.

PERSON 2

I thought that I had her there, that moment when she bent towards me. But, there was nothing – all she did was ask for more ice. We were in the midst of a typical Bombay October – a hellishly humid vestige of the monsoon gone by. It was fucking hot, especially with her lounging around in my house, playing very hard to get or just plain disinterested. It was hard to believe that she wasn't attracted to me all of a sudden – the recent vociferous sex and palpable chemistry could attest to that. Well, two can play that game. As I handed back her glass packed with ice, I said 'Need to get into something more comfortable, it's extremely hot and muggy. I'll be right back.' My one and only sexy tank-top, err, camisole, was going to come into play. Silky-soft grey, delicate spaghetti straps, sedate lace along the chest and a cut that left nothing to the imagination. My breasts practically brimmed over the neckline. I left my jeans on, the thought of her unbuckling my belt, popping the button, easing my hips out and undressing me really turned me on.

I walked out towards her with my best poker face and waited for a reaction. A long, indolent stare was thrown my way and then she was back to sipping her drink. Not a word, smile or any indication in her body language. I started to mix another round as her glass was nearing the end. It was too bad, I yearned for her – but it didn't seem like there would be any action tonight. The feeling of sexiness in my own skin, evoked by recent memories, ruminative fantasies and her tangible presence, was waning rapidly. My need, my wetness and my horniness remained unaffected.

Sitting down opposite her, stiff drink in hand, I had decided that after multiple rebuffs, I should let the night take its course. Our conversation verged on the mind-numbingly mundane – from different factions in the Bombay queer scene to talking about the best shacks in Goa. I was getting a pleasant buzz despite the setbacks in the sex department. I couldn't complain about the view either – the glorious mass of hair cut spunky short, the way that cigarettes dangled in those hands with the severely-cut nails, the outline of her nipples through that snug collared t-shirt, those dykey outdoor laced-up boots. And how could I forget the way that husky drawl prowled around my ears. So, I kept the alcohol flowing.

We were sinking our teeth into a discussion on the best place to get food after 3 a.m. in Bombay – be it egg-bhurji outside Cooper Hospital or pav-bhaji in Dadar, when she stood up abruptly. Before I could fully grasp what was happening, her knees were on my chair and sandwiched my legs tight. Her lips fell on mine as her body tilted into mine. Lips teased each other into submission as mouths made way for tongues that felt like waves lapping up against each other. Soon however, it became a roiling jumble of teeth, lips and tongue. Her knees were like pincers holding my waist in, as my thighs were spread apart.

PERSON 1

I wasn't thinking about it anymore. I just did it – Dutch courage, not to mention the sight of her in that top, showing off very hard, delectably big, round nipples. All of a sudden, my mind didn't seem to know what my body was doing, but she didn't seem to be bothered by my rushing her as she twisted her face up towards me the moment I braced my hands on the back of the chair. I adored kissing that mouth, those lips that moved in delicious ways and that expert tongue. The slow slide of my hands from her neck to her shoulders was halted by the straps of the tank-top. They felt so fragile; I wondered how they held everything in as I hooked a thumb under each side. Her hands were in my hair, tousling, ruffling and entangling. My thumbs moved downward to the sweeping curve of the breasts I'd been eyeing all night.

She moaned soft and short as I brushed her nipples with my index fingers. I let my thighs sink onto her lap, unable to hold my own weight all of a sudden. She yanked at my collar and pulled my t-shirt off. Swiftly, we were a jumble of hands, legs, tongues and undress. I could feel her nipples harden against my tongue, and harden, and harden. My body seemed to know how to talk to hers. The sofa creak, the slow whir of the fan and her deep sighs frequently punctuated our humid sex. She caught my wrist and guided my hand down to her cunt.

The nape of my neck felt the finely-wrought pressure of her tongue sucking my skin against her teeth. It was exquisite, the way she squeezed her handful of my ass. My handful of her breast – grabbed, pulled, squashed, slurped. Squelch was what her wetness felt like as my finger penetrated her. She swallowed up one finger, then two and then a third, voraciously. The groans were louder now and were reverberating inside my head. She tugged me deeper and deeper inside her as her finger skated over the folds of my clit.

PERSON 2

The morning after, the heady taste of her swished around in my mouth. Nights later, images and sensations of her fucking me lashed at my bedposts and left me unmoored. The vehement thrust of her fingers made my cunt thrum. Oh what a stupendous fuck! I couldn't wait to have a taste of the succulent mouth, the strident muskiness and that luxurious flesh again. The central-line, western-line divide of the Bombay local train was lover-girl's reason for staying away. She took a week to visit me, with a bottle of flavoured vodka and mixer in tow.

Lover-girl was wearing an air of diffidence. A summary hug, not even a peck on the cheek and a skittish seat on a narrow chair. I wondered whether I had grossly misread her. Maybe she got bored quick, after all last time it I had to pull out the camisole. So I upped the ante with outrageous flirting but she was distant. Only the drinks saw a response of unbridled enthusiasm from her. Together, we were flailing in platitudes, while inside my head I was left leching and craving. At least I had alcohol to fall back on – half of the bottle was over. I decided to call it a night and had started steering the conversation in that direction when she bent over and kissed me, squarely smack-dab on the lips, leaving no room for misinterpretation.

I drank in her nakedness while I sucked on her toes. She reached out with her other foot and pinched my nipple with her toes, making my eyes tear and my cunt wet. She played rough and I liked it. A silent submission to my savage bites on her back was chased by an abrupt flip that snatched my breath away. As she drove her fingers into me, her tongue wreaked havoc on my clit. I came – screaming, legs thrashing and fistfuls of her hair crumpling in my fists.

Sex with her left me reeling. We started having our encounters once every fortnight. A sense of deja-vu crept up on me once we started meeting regularly. Her body made me giddy. The penetration was blistering, the sex sublime but lover-girl took a while to get into the action. Was I too boring? Over-eager? The routine was religiously followed – meet at night, spend hours drinking, make platonic conversation and have sex at the end of the night. I was tiring of the routine. I wanted for her to walk in one day and push my face to the wall. I wanted to feel a warm breath on my neck, hands circle my waist and to collapse back into her with my overpowering need. One hand stimulating my nipple and the other one on my clit. The next time she came over, I would tell her my fantasy. Brandishing my boobs along with dirty talk – hopefully, that would turn her on enough to do it.

PERSON 1

She made me crazy with her moans, the way she bit her lip and her hunger to give me a blow-job. She made me nervous with the free rein she gave to her sexual being, the forthright manner in which she pursued me relentlessly from the moment I walked through her door. Always had to stave her off until I had my fill of alcohol. Her sexiness unsettled me in delicious ways and tonight would be no exception. On request, I had worn a red-and-black checked shirt for which she had professed her love.

It had been four months since we had started doing our

thing, but I was still thrown out of gear when I rang her doorbell. The hug I could manage easily, but after that, envisioning the kiss – on the lips? With tongue? Peck? On the cheek? A quick peck could be plausible when disengaging from the hug. Thinking of how to give a long and wet kiss or responding to one would always stress me out and then I ended up not doing anything at all or looking like an awkward, hasty chump while doing it.

She opened the door and grabbed my hand to pull me in. Shoving the door shut with the ball of her foot, she backed me into it. Uncertain, excited and panicky, I flattened up against it hard, feeling the eyehole press into my scalp. Sex was in the air, I could almost smell it. Two pairs of tautly-clasped hands skidded up against the door until they reached shoulder level. Her knee rose up as her toes travelled along the inner seam of my pants. Toes digging into my crotch, knee bent up against my chest, hands pushed against the wall, noses touching each other's tips.

This was so fuckin' hot. No one had ever done this to me before. Both electrified and embarrassed, I wished that I had a drink before showing up. If I had drunk enough maybe I could flip her to the wall and unzip her to fuck her. That's what the confident me could have done. Right now, I didn't know what to do with myself or how to enjoy what was happening to me – I needed to feel it all, but instead I kept on thinking. If I could get my hands on a little alcohol, my brain wouldn't get in the way of my actions. Wet, wanting but wary – I just couldn't do this.

PERSON 2

She smelled so good and looked yummy in that shirt. I wasn't going to wait around for her to jump me. Arousal coursed through me as my hand, five fingers splayed, pushed hers down against the door. I angled my foot into her crotch, ran it down her thigh and flexed it to my right. My foot pushed, her legs parted and pelvis jutted into pelvis. I had her standing spread-eagled and pinned to the wall. Hunching over her, my tongue pried open her lips almost forcefully, entering her mouth and traversing the underside of her tongue.

Lover-girl offered no resistance – silent, submissive and passive. This was my payback for all the nights of all-consuming lust – my sleep seized from me with thoughts of her fucking me, fucking me hard, fucking me long and hard. I heaved into her when I started kissing the point where the sharp jawline met the neck. Whether I kissed, licked or sucked – she tasted good all over. My cunt ached for her so, my grip on her hands slackened in the hope that they would wander.

PERSON 1

The way she kissed me on my neck made my toes curl. She had immobilised me so it was a relief that I wasn't expected to do anything. The lapel of her coat rubbed my nipple and made it hard. It was the first time I'd seen her in formal office wear. An austere, high pony-tail, a brown coat covering a sternly buttoned, stiffly starched, constricted white shirt, followed by khakis. A stunning combination, the serious, controlled exterior with a raging, out-of-control interior. I had barely begun to enjoy looking at her, when I started to think of how I would eventually have to get all of this off her. How do you divest someone of a jacket? Plus women's formal pants always seem to have three extra, unnecessary and oddly placed buttons to be unfastened.

Maybe I wouldn't have to do anything soon; this could be just a very sexy greeting. After a few drinks some random buttons wouldn't even enter my head and I wouldn't look like I didn't know what I was doing. I couldn't see the glasses nor the bottle of vodka on the counter. Uh-oh! No, not possible, she probably didn't have the time to get the bottle out. I realised that she had let go of my hands, maybe she'd had enough. But, no, she just stood there, her thigh wedged in between mine.

PERSON 2

Oh no, not the blank stare again. I stood my ground and looked into her eyes. Surely my body language was unmistakable. She remained impassive. Fuck! What was it with this woman? I kept her pinned to the door, took her hand and put it in between my breasts. She wasn't even a dogmatic top who would resent me taking the initiative. This unresponsiveness was so tough to deal with. What was it about me or what I was doing, that put her off so badly? Wouldn't any hot-blooded dyke react to my onslaught and plunder what was on offer?

Still somewhat reticent, perhaps she needed a little help from me. My fingers slid inside my lapel and moved downwards to expose my shoulder. She stood stock still, hand still resting on my chest. Sigh. But, she didn't seem to be uncomfortable, so I ran my index finger slowly along my collarbone to my shoulder and eased it out of my jacket. I did the same to my other shoulder and let my jacket fall to the floor. She didn't move a muscle, though her eyes followed the jacket falling to the floor.

PERSON 1

This was excruciating. Did she have any idea what she was doing to me? Her jacket almost slithered off her body in the sexiest way possible. She was waiting for me to continue what she started, but I just couldn't. I was about to go to pieces with mounting panic and arousal. If only she'd have waited till I had a few drinks. Unfazed by my inaction, she undid her top button. And then, the one after that, and after that too. Cleavage, then midriff and finally belly-button. I could pull her close and kiss her, but maybe she preferred me to undo her pant buttons, which would be a catastrophe.

After waiting for a moment, she decided to continue. Her thumb flicked the first button of her pants and moved away to caress her belly-button. I was mesmerised as her hand travelled up. She had started touching her breast with round strokes. Her free hand reached her other breast, her head tilted back and she fondled harder. It was driving me wild. She took two steps back, disengaging from my body. Her shirt flitted off her body and she put a hand behind her back to unclasp her bra. Was it her intention to have me watch all along? What sort of a reaction is a voyeur supposed to give? I had no clue.

PERSON 2

I was going to have to do it all and leave the wham, bam up to her. I let my bra fall to the floor. I stepped out of my pants after wrestling with all the fiddly buttons. Panties, made damp by my wetness, bunched up along my thighs as I dragged them down. Lover-girl stood rooted to the floor, I stepped towards her – stark naked. I wanted those hands to run along the length of my body, to take me in their grasp and have their way with me. Stripping for her had made my yearning worse. It also made me feel uber-sexy. I felt desperate for her touch. Surely this was enough for her – I'd never worked so hard at seducing anyone. Tonight I wasn't going to stop at anything.

PERSON 1

She stood painfully close to me, but my arms hung limp. If I exhaled she would feel my breath on her face. The smell of her shampoo punched me in the nose; her hair cascaded down onto me as she undid her high ponytail. The pressure was unbearable; I was on the verge of hyperventilating. She did want me to touch her, stroke her, finger her, fuck her. I was desperate for her but I just couldn't wrap my head around how to do it. At this point, I was ready to chug out of the bottle.

Her fingers ran down her neck and her feet were now planted apart. Dragged, pulled, pinched, her fingers ran amok – her ass, her taut nipples, sexy calves, inner thighs and in her hair. I loved the way she threw her head back and my cunt throbbed every time a sigh escaped the lips she kept on biting. Her index finger was poised just above her opening. She waited there forever. I was torn – no matter how much I wanted to, I couldn't even lift a single finger – couldn't shake the feelings of embarrassment, self-consciousness and impending doom. Her eyes flickered from my face to my hands and her finger plunged into her cunt.

She removed her finger, almost instantly and ran it along my upper lip and then my lower lip. I could have collapsed right there, but instead I tasted her wetness. Her finger made its way back down. Looking at the movements of her wrist – slow, deliberate, circular – made me tremble. I was riveted, her movements were becoming quicker, her sounds louder. She was rocking back and forth on her feet.

PERSON 2

I came tumultuously, by my own hand, panting hard. She was still standing against the door, silent. I was surprised by myself, seized by the moment, by insurmountable hunger – I had stripped and masturbated in front of another person. My reserve, my body-image issues and discomfort seemed to have melted away tonight. I was satiated for now. But, the niggling question of her passivity still bothered me. Was I not sexy enough? Why did she bother to have sex with me then? Still standing, in the same place, her face betrayed no emotion. I had gotten my release, what of her? With no reaction forthcoming, I shrugged and picked up a t-shirt from a pile of clean clothes. Lover-girl finally moved, towards my alcohol cabinet. She took out a bottle, reached for a glass and then opened the freezer for ice. This was the first independent action she had taken after stepping across the threshold.

~

Our meetings became regular over the next six months. Sometimes, my yearning for her drove me insane. She seemed to want me as much – though it was tough to tell. After so many attempts at seducing her, I had given up. We went through the same rigmarole, the same routine unfailingly – whether it was fingering, oral sex or using a dildo. It hurt me to realise that she needed to drink before committing a remotely sexual act with me. I mean, was I that bad that she needed to get drunk before she could fuck me? Without alcohol, she just wouldn't have sex – I'd denied alcohol to her a few times and had paid for it by being denied sex. I was somewhat habituated to the pre-sex rituals now, and would keep her first drink mixed and ready as she walked through the door.

Most days I would have my indignation, frustration and impatience under control, but today I was chomping at the bit. It was probably because we hadn't met for over three weeks thanks to schedules clashing and her travelling on work. I was feeling very horny but kept telling myself that

I would have to bide my time. I had plopped ice into a glass of vodka and orange juice when the doorbell rang.

PERSON 1

I was so eager to see her, this sensual woman with whom I was having outstanding sex. I was greeted with a warm hug and my first drink. She had learned along the way not to give a kiss nor expect one. It was a huge relief for me, not to have to feel that sort of pressure on seeing her. She looked gorgeous in anything. Today it happened to be an oversized shirt on boxers. It had gotten to a stage where she would wait for me to finish my drinks and make a move, rather than trying to seduce me. The arrangement seemed to work for her – she'd always be the one to ask when we were meeting next.

I was savouring my drink as we chatted about travelling and the distinctive smell of Bombay that hit as soon as one would teeter near its edges – be it train or plane. We lived in the odour, but faced it only when returning home. I loved watching her lips move as she spoke, and how her hair would get whiplashed back if it fell on her face as she talked. And I could actually enjoy the underlying simmering sexual tension between us because she was well-settled in my routine.

PERSON 2

I took one look at her and my resolve of patience flew out the window. I wouldn't mind if she unzipped me and fucked all in a welcome greeting. A new haircut, her black-rimmed spectacles, body-hugging white pants and a purple shirt – lover-girl knew how to get me where it hurt. As we spoke, I kept on telling myself to keep a lid on my galloping itch for her. But, at the same time, I wondered – for once couldn't we do it my way? For just once, I wanted spontaneous sex. I didn't want to go through the motions, complete the ritual – after all this isn't a Japanese tea ceremony.

Why was the alcohol necessary? I didn't even know that! My lack of sex, heightened arousal and sheer frustration at being compelled to have sex in a routine grated inside my head. I was working myself up to multiple passions, seething and stewing with lust, anger, indignation, wonder and desire. I couldn't handle it anymore – tonight, we'd do it my way. I'd had enough – after all, it was fair to expect some reciprocity.

PERSON 1

She didn't seem to be in a mood to talk tonight. Distracted, lost in her thoughts and distant. It had been an hour since I had reached her place, but she kept looking at her watch. I'd never seen her behave in this way. I tried mentioning some of her hot-button issues – communalism, the institution of marriage – but they failed to rouse a peep out of her. Maybe a few drinks would loosen her up. I offered to make the second round of drinks.

I was surprised by the stern 'No' from her. She usually got us the drinks, but was perfectly happy to let me do it from time to time. Shaking her head in a slow continuous movement, she made for her glassware cabinet. Our empty glasses weren't given a glance. She pulled out four shot glasses and plonked them down in front of me. With a few long, angry strides, she was back at the kitchen counter. Brandishing the vodka bottle in her hand, she halted in front of me. Taken aback by the vigour of her movements, I wondered what the deal was. Maybe she wanted to do shots … But, something was off and I couldn't tell what.

She poured the vodka into the shot glasses in one unending motion, slopping liquid over the edges. I asked her if she was alright. Again came the head-shake, 'No, I'm not alright. I can't handle it anymore. You need to drink – then it's best to get it over with. No beating around the bush tonight. Don't argue – you're going to down these one after another.' Maybe it was her voice, or the way her body was bristling with an intense energy – I chose not to question her even though I don't like my vodka in a shot.

One. Two. Three. Four. Ugh, I hated the taste in my mouth. Was this the price for good sex? She commanded me with a satisfied 'stay right there' and strode off to her cupboard. She came back to me bearing a plastic bag. Out came belts, straps and finally her shiny, black silicone dildo. Damn, were we going through this again? I thought she'd acclimatised to me. Wordlessly, she came to my chair and ran the wide belt past my ankles and knees up to my waist. The narrower straps were run up each leg and stopped at my upper thigh. She pulled at the buckles and tightened the harness to the point of eating into my flesh.

Now I was really worried, what the fuck was she doing?

Her determination was scaring me. Finally she took the dildo and attached it to the rubber ring in the middle of the harness. I was now sitting, fully clothed, on a chair in the middle of her room, wearing a seven-inch cock. Was she readying me for sex? I wasn't going to be able to do anything until the alcohol hit me. I ventured to ask what she was doing. She snarled at me in response, 'Don't worry; you won't have to do much.' She unbuttoned her shirt in a cavalier fashion – so it definitely wasn't a seduction. Her boxers wriggled off next.

Bending down to the plastic bag, she pulled out a condom wrapper. Struggling to open it, she let her teeth have a go at it. Her movements seemed calm and methodical now. In contrast, I'd begun to feel dizzy with the shots and swelling panic. She bent down to me and rolled the condom on the dildo. Standing up erect, she looked at me from top to bottom and raised an eyebrow. She raised her left leg and I felt her calf moving across my thigh. She sat on my lap – butt-naked – arms around my neck. I was freaked out but powerless to do anything. As usual, my arms hung limp by my sides.

In a slick motion she hoisted herself up and smack back down on the dildo. It was inside her – I was inside her. Her ass moved in a circle. Her eyes were locked onto mine as she continued with the slow grind. I did nothing but maintain eye-contact, I was trapped in her thrall. Her body moved a little faster as she arched upwards into me. Her chin rose slightly, a few sounds escaped her lips. She was breathing from her mouth now and I could feel it on my nose. Her breasts jiggled near my face. She propped her hands on my shoulder-blades and her nails dug into me as she starting battering me furiously. Grazing my face, her breasts made a soft thump sound as they smacked back into her body. Toes on the floor, her kickboxer's calves were pummelling with all their might. Noisy moans. Dripping sweat. Hair wrenching. Chair rocking unsteadily. Teeth gnashing. Shuddering. Climaxing uproariously. I'm still inside her now unmoving, limp body, collapsed against mine – whose arms still hang limply.

Soliloquy

Chicu

I stand damp and tousled in front of my cupboard. *The pink synthetic,* I decide. For whatever reason, my body wants to be seen today. *And why not,* I think as I discard the towel. I have earned these curves. They may come naturally to some, but they are the result of hard work for me. I gaze into the mirror with satisfaction at the gentle spread of my hips. My breasts are goose-pimpled from the shower, my nipples taut. *Oh yes, show them off.* I wink at myself.

My dress and make up routine is meticulous as always. A chikan bra and pretty panties are followed by a crisply-ironed petticoat and blouse. The ritual of draping a sari soothes me and my confidence increases with each careful pleat. Draping the pallu takes a lot of attention. It must be just so. Not revealing enough to attract censure, but not hiding the curves I am proud of. The last safety-pin is in place. I give myself a critical look in the mirror. I check the back to see if the sari is riding up and note approvingly the brief hint of a dark waist behind the sheer pink material.

Satisfied with the sari, I turn my attention to my hair. It is growing well now. I take pleasure in combing it out before gathering it into a prim bun.

Now for the icing on the cake: make-up and accessories. I smile like a little girl playing with her treasure chest as I sort through my assorted bits of sunshine. I choose earrings, bangles, and a slim necklace. My fingers graze the silver anklets and I hesitate. Was it Coco Chanel who said that when accessorizing one should always take off the last thing one put on? I wear them anyway. Forgetting my care for the carefully-draped pleats, I hitch up my sari and bounce on my feet listening to the jingle of the bells. I look up and laugh with the delighted girl I see in the mirror. The pink frosted lipstick I choose reflects my sunny mood. A swipe of kajal is followed by a dusting of powder. *Never forget to powder your ears*, I remember my adopted mother saying.

My adopted mother. It seems false to say that. After all, she gave birth to the woman I see in the mirror; gave me the permission to be who I always was. I cannot fault my birth mother either. After many girls, she finally gave birth to a boy. The family was elated, and many plans were made for the little heir. When she discovered my penchant for dressing in my sisters' clothes, her distress was understandable. In an attempt to dissuade me, she boxed my ears when she found me using her make-up. I thought then that she was ashamed of me. Later, I realized she was also afraid for me. She wanted to spare her child pain. She suffered when the neighbours tutted about me; she suffered even more when her husband beat her for giving birth to a defective son.

Most of all, she was anguished when he – my father – threatened to beat me into submission. Her punishments were milder than those he threatened to inflict on me. Naturally, she wanted to correct my behaviour before he took that job upon himself. It was not in her to understand that for me, the pain of living as a man was a torture far worse than her beatings. She meant well, but she left me with no option but to run away. What else could I do? I was tired of the beatings and the ridicule. I was tired of seeing my mother being punished for who I was. Running away was so easy! A walk 'to the market', an exchange of some money for a rail ticket, and I soon found myself in a city large enough to provide me with anonymity. Sadly, a city that is generous with its anonymity is stingy with its welcome. Here too, I was cursed with being between worlds. Being from a 'good family' I could not bring myself to beg, but at the same time that family did not have place for me. My money ran out fast, and I found myself without shelter and food. And it was then that Amma found me. Starving, delirious with fever, with the earrings I had stolen from my mother clenched in my fist.

'If you get better, I will pierce your ears so that you can wear them,' she promised me as I struggled against the healing poultices she applied on my chest. She followed through on that promise, and on many more. The only payment she extracted was an unquestioning obedience. I was not the only one in Amma's care. I found myself with other women like me, all allowed to live the way they were meant to be. The other women followed a fairly stereotypical career; singing and dancing at peoples' houses and more or less coercing them into parting with their money. For me, Amma had something different in mind. 'You are not like them,' she said. 'You are posh. You are a graduate. People listen to you. You should work in an office; we need someone like that.' I was happy enough to agree. I worked as a typist and did Amma's chores whenever she needed someone 'posh' to negotiate the world for her. I only protested when she told me to leave the house and live elsewhere. 'There is nothing more I can do for you,' she told me. 'Go out now, beti. Live the way you want to live. Come and visit your Amma, but live outside.' She was right. Hormone therapy and Amma's training had made me all the woman I could be. The operation to complete the transformation from man to woman is not within my reach and probably will never be. I do not mind too much. This is enough for me. I am happy, I am free. As for the odd hidden secret, who does not have one?

I finish applying my make-up. As I take a last look in the mirror, my elated mood disappears. I recollect what I go through once I step out of the doors that protect me now. I feel the speculative glances on my body, hear the whispers. I see myself brushing past the leering crowd with my head lowered as if in submission. It is not lenient, this world of mine. It reminds me over and over again that I am vulnerable, forcing me to dig deep within for my reserves of strength. Every day, I return depleted to sleep alone in my little room. I always wonder what it would be like to have someone to return to. Would we hurry back home together? Shutting the world out would no longer be merely a relief, it would be a joy. Home would not mean just a place to hide, but a sanctuary in every sense of the word. But would it really be like that, I ask myself. I think of the people I know who are as trapped in their relationships as I am outside of one. I don't care. I want my chance. I want to know what it feels like.

The clock reminds me I am running late. As I rush out, my face assumes the wooden expression it reserves for masking vulnerability.

~

My body aches from being stretched out as I am. My hands clench the iron bars above me as my feet desperately strain to retain their grip on the floor. I do not really need to hold on to the bars bolted to the roof; the loops around my wrists will support me well enough even if I were to completely let go. But it would be an admission of defeat to slump in my position. Despite the sweat making my hands slippery, I hold on.

The man in front of me shifts a step backwards, fitting his body to mine. He stands with his back exposed to my scrutiny. He is not an attractive man from this angle, our proximity a matter of his choice rather than mine. The cheap nylon shirt he wears stretches across his shoulders and accentuates their roundness. What I can see of his cheeks makes me realise they are round too. I can see every hair follicle, the creases in his neck. His ears are smooth and surprisingly shiny. He has oiled his hair, and I fancy I can trace the path where some of the oil has gone below the nape of his neck. This intimate gazing upon him overwhelms me and I shut my eyes.

I cannot shut him out though; he has positioned himself too well. Suspended as I am, moving backwards is not an option. Even if it were, I have nowhere to go. The woman behind me now has rested her head on my shoulder. I am not happy with this intimacy and turn my face away from her. I attempt to show my displeasure by shrugging a shoulder, but I cannot shake her off without breaking the rules. For the same reason, I cannot simply knee the man in front of me. I do not make eye contact with either of them, refusing to acknowledge their existence. These rules make me laugh even as I follow them. It seems to me as though the only contact that is not allowed is that of eye to eye. Nothing else is a violation. Breasts are groped and buttocks pressed against genitals; anything is permissible as long as it is done without a nod to the other's humanity.

The three of us stand there, pressed against each other. My eyes still closed, I force myself to relax. There is no shame here, I tell myself. This place is outside judgement. It does not matter who I am, who I consider myself to be, who others see me as. All that matters is being here, all that matters is accepting the moment.

I slowly go through the various sensations surrounding me. I inhale deeply. The salty and slightly sour smell of the man in front of me is all I notice first. Almost immediately after, I notice that this dominant note is overlain with the sweetness of the oil he has used on his hair and the metallic smell of the iron bars around me. I cannot smell the woman behind me. This bothers me. She is a part of my world too. I am driven by an urgent need to feel her olfactory presence.

She is leaning against my shoulder, and I turn my head to catch a whiff of her breath. It is warm and strangely sweet. It takes a moment before the cause of the sweetness registers. The woman has been eating mangoes. I am reassured by this. I like mangoes for breakfast too. This is a woman who eats and lives, not just a looming shadow.

I continue with my inventory of sensations and come to touch. Here, it is the woman who dominates my universe. Her breasts are pressed against my back. With every breath, I feel her nipples stroke my skin. She is grabbing the bars to either side of me, enclosing me in the warm cage of her embrace. More than her breasts, it is the caress of her arms that feels intimate. This closing in should make me feel claustrophobic, but it does not. Instead, I feel safe, wrapped in security. As long as her arms are around me, no one else can approach. I feel her breath against my neck. It is warm and moist, but leaves a cool sensation. I enjoy the gift of her caressing breath. Then it occurs to me to give the same pleasure I am receiving. I acknowledge to myself that even in this unexpected and anonymous grouping, even in this short span of time, I have developed my favourites. I am more interested in the man in front of me than I am in the hugging woman behind. I want to tease him, to impress my presence on him. It is he who shall receive the gift of my attentions. I have an image of walking home with a man. I want it to be real. I know this is not where that dream will come true, but I cannot resist being attracted to this man.

I incline my head towards him ever so slightly. I know that my breath is leaving a cooling trail on his neck. I begin to control my breathing and let each slow exhalation rake its way across his skin. His stance becomes rigid, and I sense that he is afraid to move lest he miss a single caress. This knowledge makes me bolder. I purse my lips and trace the outline of his ear with my breath. I am rewarded with a shuddering sigh and he backs into me.

It is all I can do to not rest my chin on his shoulder. Is this what it feels like to spoon with someone, I wonder. Like he did only a few minutes earlier, I stand still. Like a woman enchanted by the trusting approach of a bird, I am scared to breathe lest the moment end. For a long while, we stand quietly. The ache in my arms is forgotten. All I can feel is the wonderful warmth of another body resting against mine. I open my eyes and study him as he stands there. He is not unattractive, I realise. He is real. Uncomfortable with the situation, I had only seen the negative in him. Now I see a hardworking and simple man who tries to make the best of what he has. I rein my thoughts in and laugh at myself. I won't see this man again. We are thrown together by chance. He is not a soul-mate. I scold myself out of my fantasies and bring my thoughts back to the present.

He is pressing against me now, his buttocks hard against that most private part of me. I wonder if he is thinking of what lies underneath the softly-draped sari. I wonder if he is aroused at the thought of entering me, of being enclosed in a protective embrace. I am suddenly uncomfortable as I realise the gap between his fantasy and my reality. I lean into him, shifting my pelvis away. My breasts press against him, and I let them grind against his back. This will take his mind off his earlier quest, I reason. My secret will be uncovered when and how I choose. I will decide the time, the place, and the person to whom I reveal myself.

For a few minutes, my plan of offering my breasts to the man works, and he ceases to grind against me. But soon, his old search begins. Despite my dodging, his buttocks graze against me once, once more, and yet again. On the pretext of shifting his footing, he moves into me. The woman behind, whose touch and breath I so enjoyed, has left me no place to move. He presses against me once again and all at once I have no more secrets. His gasp and the sudden stiffening of his back dispel all my illusions. He hesitates and then presses against me again. His body slowly and discreetly grinds against mine. But I have now lost the pleasure I took in our game. This uncovering of my secret feels like a public disrobing. I feel exposed, dirty, ashamed. I want it all to end.

I seek a way to leave and just above me I see my lifeline. Loosening my hold on the overhead bar, I grab the rope and give it a quick yank. I hear that sharp *ting* with relief.

The driver hears it too and the bus rolls to a stop. I mutter a quiet – and hypocritical – 'Excuse me, bhaisaab,' and make my way through the crowded aisle to the exit, my head inclined downwards. Not once do my eyes meet those of the other passengers. Good girls like those I resemble do not make eye contact with men. There is one man on that bus however, who knows that I am not what I seem. I do not look at him either. I do not want to look into the eyes of the stranger with whom I have played an illicit game and see his shock. Still, shock would not be the worst. The worst would be to see disgust in his eyes. I will not look up, I decide. I know where I am, I don't need landmarks to guide me. I will keep my eyes on the road and walk demurely to the office. Let those who notice think my face is flushed because of the exertion.

I step off the bus determined to walk off, but then hesitate. I look up at the bus. There is one passenger standing where I was, staring at me. One passenger with slightly oily hair and clad in a synthetic shirt. I see no revulsion in those eyes, only a shared knowledge and a shared desire. The bus begins to pull away and I realise I was wrong. The worst thing I could see in his eyes is not disgust. It is pain and bewilderment. He continues to look at me even as I stare hungrily back. Then the bus is gone and I am devastated.

I straighten my shoulders, and gather my pallu about me. I am not defeated. There is next time. He will be back. He will be in the same bus again, hoping to find me. I saw it in his eyes. And I will be there. I step around a puddle, careful not to muddy my sari. I will be wearing it again tomorrow.

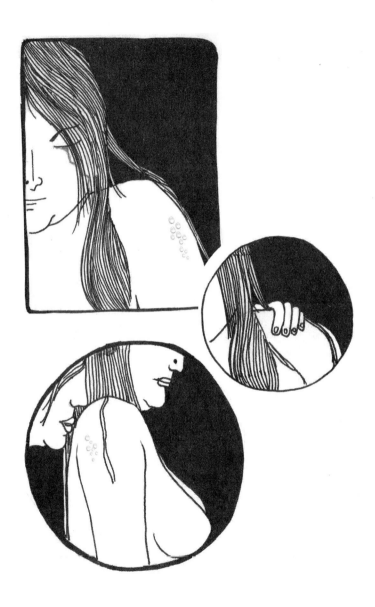

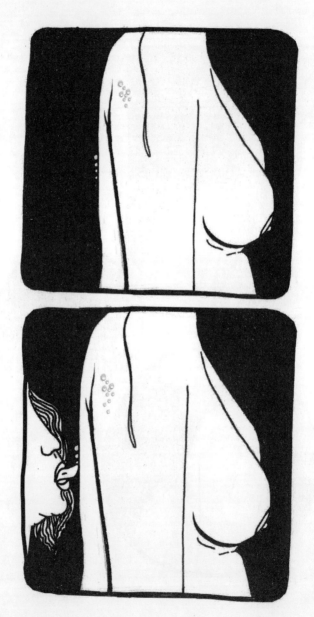

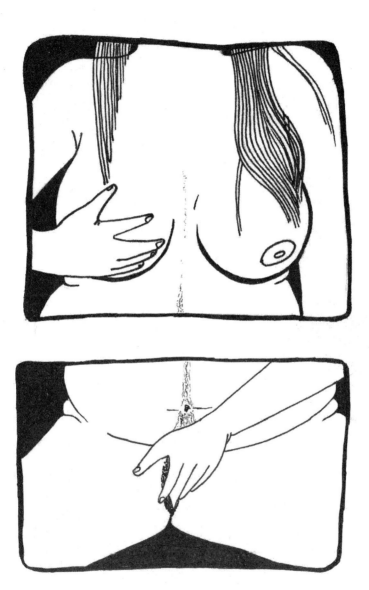

The Marriage of Somavat and Sumedha

Devdutt Pattanaik

If the queen had seen them naked, she would have known they were both boys, exceedingly beautiful boys, virgins, eager for marriage.

She would have especially appreciated Somavat with his large languid eyes, and his irresistibly charming smile. But a layer of creamy turmeric cleverly masked the roughness of his face. Drapes of red fabric hid the expanse of his chest. His manhood, thick and long, envied by all those who saw it wet in the village pond, was firmly tucked in by an extremely tight loincloth. All the queen of Vallabhi saw was a short, stocky, rather awkward bride leaning against tall Sumedha of the serene face, sonorous voice, silken hair, and graceful walk. To her eyes, these two were husband and wife, a young couple, seeking her blessings and her cow, not childhood friends who loved to wrestle on wet riverbanks.

~

Imposters! That's who they are! The royal cow, Nandini, saw through the bridal disguise the instant she was handed over. She noticed the groom's hesitation as he bowed to the queen, and the hurried gait of the bride as they walked out of the palace. She lowed in protest, but no one understood what she was saying.

This would not do. The pious queen could not be fooled. The sky grumbled with thunderclouds in acknowledgement. A drop of angry rain fell to the ground. The trees hissed. The boys wanted to hurry, but the cow refused to cooperate. She hoped the guardians of the city would bare their fangs, catch the deceivers and castrate them.

~

Unaware of the cow's frothing fury, Somavat and Sumedha walked on either side of the cow, placing their hands on her tawny back, their fingers brushing occasionally in reassurance and relief.

Orphans since childhood, they had always relied on each other for support. Together they ate, together they bathed, and together they washed the sacred utensils in the temple courtyard. Together they understood the meaning of the songs that the courtesan sang before the deity on festive nights. Together they dreamt of the dark voluptuous nymphs described in epics, whose walk caused the jasmine to bloom all day and whose dance distracted sages all night. Together they figured out why bulls leap over cows, why snakes coil around each other, and why bewildered dogs walked in pairs in the middle of the street trapped at the genitals. Together they peeped into homes and discovered how the clumsy priest made love to his clumsier wife, and why the rich merchant grunted every time his young wife, his third, buried her head between his ample thighs. Together they learnt what makes a boy a man and a man, a husband.

Eager for brides, they had spoken to the village elders and were told, 'Earn yourself a cow, and we will find you wives.' But who would give a cow to orphans? Desperate, they had hatched this plan to dupe the kind queen of Vallabhi, famous for giving cows to newly-wedded couples.

It was Somavat's plan; he always took the lead. Sumedha always followed. He had long accepted that Somavat was the smarter one, who always knew what to do. Besides, Somavat got annoyed if anyone told him what to do. Only this time he was not too happy: he had to dress like a woman and walk behind Sumedha – he was shorter, rounder, and cuter, as Somavat pointed out, enjoying his dominating friend's discomfort.

~

The plan had worked. Sumedha remembered the affection of the queen as she welcomed them into her royal courtyard, washed their feet, offered them food, and wished them a hundred children as she handed over the cow. But uneasiness gripped his heart, guilt snaked its way in. What they had done was wrong!

Wrong? A mission spawned in poverty. Surely the gods understood. Surely the queen would understand. Sumedha grabbed Somavat's hand, painted red, firmly. There was comfort in those hands. Somavat squeezed Sumedha's fingers, a gentle acknowledgment of his friend's anxiety, and continued walking. They had the cow, they had left the city, soon they would reach the village, get wives and all would be okay. They had done nothing wrong.

~

The bond between the boys touched Nandini's heart. No, no punishment for the desperate, just a twist in cosmic laws to turn this trick into truth ...

The fields gave way to the forest. The royal highway continued straight east but the boys turned into a narrow path that made its way into a thick bush. The trees made way for the imposter bride, the imposter groom and the very real cow. They then leaned back so that no one from the highway saw any trace of them. They were guests of the forest-goddess, Aranyani, who had heard the lowing of the cow and had chuckled to herself. Yes, Nandini's wish would be granted. In Aranyani's wild realm, the rules of the city evaporate like camphor: no husband, no wife, no king, no queen, no man, no woman ... only predators and prey, and the occasional lover. She sighed at the infinite possibilities of nature.

~

As they neared the cave where Somavat's clothes were hidden, Sumedha realized the cow would separate them forever. She would make them eligible for wives; with wives would come separate kitchens, separate homes, separate children and separate responsibilities. The temple would still be the same, but everything would change. He felt his skin being torn from his flesh, his breath being separated from his chest. The pain, this deep intense pain of separation, was unbearable. He walked around the cow, to get closer to friend and hugged him from behind, resting his head on his friend's shoulder. Cheek met cheek, a deep longing expressed itself.

This was not the needy hug that Somavat experienced many a time as they slept under the same blanket on winter nights. This was not the mischievous hug he had experienced in the city when Sumedha pretended to be his husband. This was different, more anxious, more demanding, a child afraid of losing his mother.

Somavat felt Sumedha's heart pounding. Why was his friend so scared? The ordeal was over; the cow had been obtained. Somavat reached out and caressed his friend's face ever so gently, his affection pouring out. He, too, was sensing the end of childhood. No longer students, they would be householders, husbands and fathers. Is this the heartache people describe when it is time to let go? Was this what was bothering Sumedha?

Somavat turned around and cupped Sumedha's face in his hands. Were those tears? Yes, his friend was crying. The realisation of the end. He hugged Sumedha tight and let his tears roll down too. Years of emotions poured out. They clung to each other, afraid of the world beyond. Between them was the only security they ever knew.

~

How does a wife comfort a frightened husband? Does she hold him tight between her breasts? Does she become mother for a moment, gently nudge him to take charge, feel powerful? Or does she become a flirtatious nymph and wipe away fear with a giggle? Somavat decided to become the nymph. No, a clown who mimics nymphs. That would make Sumedha smile once agin. He sniffed away his tears, undid the knot of his sari, twirled around with an exagerrated giggle and let the red sari unravel. 'What will people say!' he said, fluttering his eyelashes in mock shame, and ran into the cave in his loincloth, arms crossed across his chest, his sari trailing behind him. Sumedha couldn't help but smile, Somavat was so funny.

It was then he noticed Somavat's skin, bronze in the sunlight, his painted palms and soles like the flowers of the palasha tree being blown by the wind. And something changed.

A company of parrots burst forth from a jamun tree, the sound of their feathers like the exhalation of Kama's breath after he shoots a love-dart. Sumedha felt a stirring that he had never felt before. He noticed the muscles of his friend's thighs and calves as he ran into cave. He had this intense desire to touch his friend, feel the firmness of his body, smell his skin, run his hands down his back. What was this feeling? Why was it so strong?

~

Sumedha entered the cave. It was dark and cold. Somavat sat on the rock under which lay his clothes, removing his earrings. Sumedha could not explain the excitement in his heart. He had this urge to hold his friend in his arms. Blood rushed up his neck. His ears felt warm. What was this feeling? This impatient urge?

The cow sensed the change of mood. She stood at the mouth of the cave, watching the loveplay unfold.

Sumedha walked up to Somavat and held out his hand. 'What?' asked Somavat. Sumedha continued to hold out his hand. Somavat accepted it and allowed himself to be hauled up into his friend's arms. Sumedha sighed, embracing Somavat tightly.

What was going on? Somavat decided to indulge his friend.

Sumedha caressed Somavat's arms slowly, gently kneading his muscles at times. The smell of turmeric filled his nose. He rested his head on his friend's shoulder and then, very slowly, very deliberately, let his tongue trace the side of Somavat's neck. The taste of sweat and flowers filled his mouth. They fuelled his appetite.

What was this? What was Sumedha doing? It felt so good. Somavat gasped, and waited impatiently to feel Sumedha's tongue on his skin once more.

There it was, a wet line along his shoulders. There it was, a soft bite. Now, a firm bite. This felt so good.

The cow lowed. Somavat stopped. The friends turned to look. Outside a pair of peacocks were dancing, no peahen in sight. Both chuckled, sounding almost relieved. They were alone. It was all okay.

~

Sumedha returned to licking Somavat's neck. He felt like a bee having its first taste of nectar. The feeling was heady. He kept moving his hands up and down Somavat's arm. The bangles were an obstacle. 'Take these off,' he rasped, his tongue now probing into Somavat's ears.

'What?' Somavat asked.

'This,' said Sumedha pulling off the bangles. 'And this,' he said, yanking off the armlet. 'And this,' he said, tearing the garlands.

Somavat did not resist. He had never seen Sumedha so forceful, so demanding, so impatient. He felt ... wanted. Alive. Sumedha bent down to trace his lips with his tongue. Somavat parted his lips like the petals of a lotus unfolding when touched by the first light of dawn.

Outside, rain clouds rumbled. Drops of rain hit the ground. The kiss was firm, warm, affectionate. Somavat remained still as Sumedha, now emboldended, showered his face with kisses. The cold rocks of the cave suddenly felt warm and wonderful. Streams of pleasure burst forth from every corner and created a deluge of ecstasy. For once, Somavat did not know what to do.

~

Sumedha ingored the doubts that rose like demons in the fringes of his mind. He trusted this intense inexplicable urge. He slipped his fingers under the fabric of Somavat's loincloth. He felt the throbbing of Somavat's manhood. Very gently, and patiently he untied the knot. The organ curled out eagerly, delightfully stiff and joyful. Sumedha kissed his friend's chin, his neck, his chest; he lowered himself, drawing his tongue down to the navel, to the nakedness below.

Whirlpools of sensations spread out from Somavat's groin, spreading along the sides, shooting up right into his heart. He felt a happiness he had never known before. Sumedha felt completeness in his mouth. The taste of his friend's body covered his tongue. He felt the sweetness of mango down his throat. The rain outside was not enough to quench his thirst. He felt parched, giddy like a greedy bumblebee.

Finally, Somavat moved his hips in response, ready to grab some of the pleasure that he was being given. He ran his fingers through his friend's hair. He felt his hunger, and enjoyed being consumed. Sumedha's passion had enveloped Somavat's being. He stopped Sumedha. If this continued, he would burst. This moment would pass. It had to be streched. More importantly, this display of love, this joy, had to be reciprocated.

~

Lowering himself, Somavat kissed Sumedha, lip on lip, peck for peck, like doves around grain. The two friends explored every corner of each other's mouth, feeling each other's breath, hungry for the sweetness of lips and tongues and teeth, puckering and probing, sometimes ferociously, sometimes tenderly, letting love flow from one to the other. This was like a new game in the secret playground of Aranyani. It was full of delight.

Water poured rhythmically from the heavens, bringing music to the mood. The wetness from the sky made the green trees merge with the red earth. Sumedha and Somavat, dry and intimate in their cave, looked like Manu and Shatrupa, the only survivors of the deluge. The last couple. The first couple.

~

Sumedha's hand gripped the curve of Somavat's buttock. Somavat let out a sigh and buried his head in Sumedha's neck. Sumedha's fingers moved down, he felt Somavat's navel. Somavat let out a soft moan. Sumedha bored his finger deeper into the navel. Somavat moaned once again.

He rolled over Sumedha, wanting to take charge as usual, undoing his dhoti, his loincloth, spreading out his arms and legs. Sumedha's tall, lithe body looked beautiful, stretched out on the ground. Somavat stood up and watched Sumedha's eagerness call to him. The gentle tuft of hair stretching from Sumedha's navel down to his manhood reached out in anticipation. The desire to possess and be possessed consumed him. His buttocks twitched, his thighs quivered. Somavat waited for a bit, staring at his friend's body. So many times had they bathed naked in the village pond. But never had he experienced this raw urge spreading like a forest fire across his five senses.

Sumedha could not bear this teasing. Come, come, his flesh screamed, until Somavat finally lowered himself. The falling raindrops saw the white dhoti and the red sari intertwined like serpents, and atop them, the two boys holding each other, their brown bodies merging into one.

~

Sumedha looked into his friend's eyes, their intensity enhanced by the rain-smudged lampblack lining. His jaw looked firm. Coarse stubble peeped trough the turmeric. He felt his strength, his passion, his determination. He spread his legs, wanting to accommodate his friend comfortably. He wrapped them around Somavat's waist, not wanting to let his friend go, feeling his eager stiffness against Somavat's belly. He ran his fingers through Somavat's hair while Somavat bit his arm in excitement. Something about the pain that followed, and the red mark left behind, made it all real.

The sounds of lovemaking emerging from the cave excited the trees in the forest. Branches entangled with each other, while vine tendrils gripped the trunks more firmly. The forest-goddess let her thighs part to make room for the rivulets of passion sent down by the sky-gods.

~

Somavat wanted his friend to hold him tight, squeeze him, make him feel more wanted and more alive; he wanted to be the wife if that was what Sumedha desired, and husband too, if that was what he wished. Family and friend, husband and wife, these were just words. All he wanted was to be wrapped in the same skin, make Sumedha feel what he sensed.

'Lovemaking is about pleasuring the other and finding happiness in their pleasure,' the village courtesan had once said in passing. 'Thoughts,' she repeatedly stated, 'are the enemies of lovemaking, interfering with passion, emotions, sensations, annoyingly seeking patterns and explanations and justifications. Banish them when the beloved is in your arms.' Somavat and Sumedha dutifully banished all thoughts from the mind and devoured each other's being, determined to make the other happy. Mounds of flesh rose and fell. Hands multiplied as lovers tried to feel more of each other's flesh. Mouths multiplied to lick and bite and kiss more skin. Thrust followed thrust, forceful entries through open welcoming gateways, a rush of passion, turbulent juices, probing fingers, eager limbs. They clung to each other like serpents mating, arms and legs intertwined.

Their identities were lost. Somavat and Sumedha mingled and merged into each other. One ran his tongue on the inside of the other's thigh. The other turned around and let the one move his fingers across his back, down his spine, to coax the softness down below. The inside welcomed the outside. The husband's body opened up as a wife's. And the wife felt the tenderness of the most affectionate husband. The world did not exist after that, every grain of sand, every rock, every blade of grass washed away by the waters of Pralaya, but the two were together, groaning and gasping, feeling each other's breath and heartbeat, safe in each other's arms, oblivious of everything, cradled upon a floating banyan leaf.

~

The rain stopped.

The sun burst through the trees and entered the cave as a golden shaft. Butterflies, sent by Aranyani, rose from the bushes and began to dance. The queen's cow watched with amusement the imposters transformed into a real couple. Kama smiled from behind the rocks. Yama recorded it all. For this was desired, and destined.

All in the Game

Iravi

First, my arms are tied down. Then the blindfold.

'Is it tight enough?' asks Mandira.

'It's a bit too tight,' I venture.

'Who asked you?' says Ruchi. 'Just speak when you're spoken to.' Rough-gently yanking the knot so my head is pulled back. There's a nervous titter – Vini? I'm not sure, but I subside obediently. Ruchi tests the blindfold, runs a finger expertly – it seems to me – between my cheek and the taut cloth first on one side then the other and says, 'I think that's fine, it shouldn't come loose midway. Okay sweetie, you want another half-drink? Before we start? I'll hold the glass for you.' Tanu scoffs, 'Such niceness! You are just not happening as a dominatrix!'

I've had a couple of slow Bloody Marys and am just mildly buzzed. Ordinarily, another drink would be welcome, but I don't want to be too swimmy; I'm going to need my senses to be sharp – as sharp as the taste of the crushed salt from the frosted glass rim still lickable on my lips. Someone's in for a treat. Eyes closed behind the blindfold, arms strapped to armrests, I say that we can start.

There's whispering, then suddenly loose fabric brushes my knee. A kurta or a dupatta or a skirt. That rules out Vini, who's wearing a tucked-in shirt. Tanu's dupatta and Neerja's scarf are doing duty as restraints on my wrists, and I don't think their tops are all that long or loose. But I don't have too much time to think through any of this consciously: two fingers placed below my chin tilt my face up, a hand comes to rest lightly on my shoulder and ice-cool lips press against mine ... then almost at once a tongue tip flickers across the hollow between my lips, prising them minimally open. I let the tip of my own tongue greet my kisser's and a tiny current passes between us, its charge building up as we explore each other tentatively and then more decisively before the other tongue is suddenly withdrawn, the person straightens up, and crazy cheers and whoops fill the room.

'Come on, Jo – guess who?' That's Mandira asking. I think, that was either Mandira herself, who's in a skirt, or Bins or Abhay. But Mandira's on some medication and is drinking green tea, and this person's lips were ice-cube – or chilled-beer – cold. It wasn't Ruchi because I got a good whiff of her bestest-itr-e-gil-bought-in-Lucknow-during-the-conference while she was blindfolding me, and there was no heady wet earth after the first rains in my nostrils just now. No aftershave either, so it probably wasn't Abhay, who's unusually in a kurta today, but maybe he isn't wearing any cologne? 'Bins?' I say. I sense though I cannot see the conspiratorial smiles and I hear shushing gestures, then Vini intones as she writes the log – 'Num-ber *One*. Jyots-na guess-es Ben-*ai*-fer.'

Bins pipes up, 'Assuming that was me, I hope it was a good kiss. Was it?'

'Too brief,' I complain. 'And it stopped just when it was getting somewhere.' Tanu says, 'You know the rules, J. No lingering beyond the time limit.'

'And no – umm – hitting below the neck,' adds Neerja, quite gratuitously in my opinion. Rules indeed! You'd think we'd been doing this forever, instead of it being only the second time, and the first was nearly seven months ago. But lesbians learn quickly, and have long memories. Not that Abhay is a lesbian or even a woman. And Ruchi is always reminding everyone that she's this marginalised-among-the-marginalised bisexual, while Neerja likes to grandly or wistfully refer to herself as HLT (short for Hothead Paisan Homicidal Lesbian Terrorist). Most of us really just call ourselves queer when we have to call ourselves something. Certainly this is one hell of a queer game we're playing.

~

So, a brief look at the others in the cast. Mandira, architect: recovering from a bad breakup, a bit of a health-food freak. Vini (given name Vinita) and Neerja (HLT): in a relationship, a fact they refrain from advertising on FB; our only live-in lovers. Tanusri: quintessential Bangla girl-next-door who sings Rabindrasangeet while cooking machher jhol and poshto, not that you should take me too seriously. Benaifer: works in her parents' furniture store in what the newspapers, indifferent to the vast public oblivion regarding the term, persist in calling SoBo. Bins and Tanu were an item for a while, and may still be for all anyone knows. But do you really care yet about who does what or who does who, dear reader? Although, as a good or trying-to-be-good feminist I should certainly tell you about myself: I'm a gambler, and my favourite colour is . . . oh well.

Vini says, businesslike, 'Jo? Score please.' Thinking that it's bound to get much better than this, and how I can't go higher than ten even for the most knock-out ones, I say, apologetically, 'Four.'

'*Baap re*, fail score *ho gaya yeh to*!'* Bins wails, 'Oh I am so devastated! In case that was me-ee!'

'It's okay, calm down, people. Some of us just might get a second chance later.' Whispers, huddles, giggles, rustles, the plonk of ice cubes, an sms beep. Ruchi asks, 'Ready for next?' and I nod.

~

This one's a no-brainer. But oh, how soon I wish the rules could be abandoned! Both my arms are loosely gripped above the elbow as strands of hair rain on my cheeks, ears and throat, and the world becomes a teasing softness of full lips – and not-so-soft nips. The vodka's kicking in, or the kiss is pumping up the high, or is it her shampoo that's suddenly overwhelming my senses? I long to run my fingers through that green apple cloud but the restraints hold; she takes command of my lower lip and I surrender absolutely to the expert ministrations of lips and teeth and tongue.

---

*'Oh no, this score is a fail!'

'Forty-five seconds!' calls Vini. 'Time's up.' A last bite, quick and hard, before my tormentor straightens up, her hair leaving, I'm fairly certain, burn marks on my skin. I have to catch the moan that rises to my throat and change it to a cough, which probably fools nobody.

'Here, Jo, have some water.' I take a small sip then a bigger gulp from the glass held to my mouth. Then someone says, 'Hey! This is like a wine tasting or like those fancy seven-course meals. We should have a taste-changer in between!'

'Please! It's called a palate cleanser.'

'Oh yes, good idea! She has to have one, otherwise the kisses will all get mixed up.' After some debate, a piece of plain roasted papad is popped into my mouth and, after a quick google consultation, a consensus sip of soda with a dash of nimbu ('sparkling water with a twist of citrus') to remove all aftertastes and prepare me for the next round.

'We should do this in style next time – have those sorbets and all.'

'I know, like in *Julia* – uff that dining table scene when Lillian Hellman visits Julia's family, it's just unforgettable.'

'Quite a queer film, na? Although what do you make of that scene in a restaurant or something where this guy calls them lesbians and they slap him?'

'Arre! Could we not discuss a film that like 2.5 people have seen, and get back to Jo and the score card?'

~

But before I get a chance to declare, confidently, 'Tanu, seven' amid gasps and wows, there's an intense discussion about how the film was made in '70s Hollywood for fuck's sake, let's go by the subtext, yaar ... and if being in the closet means having Dashiell Hammett as your boyfriend, maybe that's not such a bad trade-off ... and anyway being called lesbians or lesbos or lovers by homophobic morons is reason enough to punch them in the nose (or wherever), no matter if you're queer or straight, and how under such circumstances you are under no compulsion to affirm or deny anything. Just as when some probable-wife-beater-and-loud-talker-on-cell-phone-during-the-film screams 'Go back to Pakistan!' at you because you refused to stand when the national anthem was forced down your throat in a movie theatre, the last thing the creep needs to know is whether or not you are Muslim. Although actually, *actually*, he does need to know; he needs to know more than he was ever taught in school or at his grandmother's knee, but do *you* want to be the one to engage with said creep? And then it's back to *Julia* and someone promises to get hold of a DVD so we can watch it together at the first opportunity. I listen, and concur, though two-thirds of me is still caught up in Tanusri's tresses. It's only when I suggest that they should untie and un-blindfold me now, and re-blindfold me when we're ready, that we resume. The high has almost worn off, but I promise myself a Bloody Mary later; meanwhile, the taste is sufficiently changed or the palate adequately cleansed and – unexpected bonus – the intellect suitably stimulated.

'Yay, Number Three, go for it!'

'Pucker up, Jyotsna!'

Vini's laptop is, absurdly, playing *switti switti switti tera pyar chaida* – on an evening that has already paid tribute to

Joan Baez, Mehdi Hasan and Amy Winehouse. Nothing else happens for what seems like a long time – Number Three appears to be diffident. Then warm palms cup my face and a nose rubs mine. This, I think, has got to be one of the self-avowed monogamous ones, who are not serious participants, but please, what's in a less eskimoesque kiss between friends?

~

Ohhh I was so wrong, or the monogamous one has read my mind – or my lips, or my libido, or something: anyway the nose knows what it's doing, as it travels like a feather all over my face in little waves and circles, over my eyelids through the blindfold, inside my ear and around its edges and down the line of my jawbone, first on one side then the other, then via the dimple on my chin to the hollow of my throat . . . yes like a feather, but also like the nose it is, tip a little roughened by peeling dry skin, sometimes lightly tracing sometimes pressing down firmly and I am loving the rough with the smooth . . . I want it to go places and do things, and everywhere it leaves a tickle of quick warm breath that's making my own breath come quicker, till it ends with a flourish, skimming my lips from right to left then back again then pausing dead centre like a performer taking a bow and awaiting the audience's verdict.

I give the nose a quick lick of appreciation, then open my mouth wide and snap in a mock attempt to bite it off. There's frantic applause. 'Wow, er – Number Three! Where did you learn *that*?' asks someone, and I imagine the nose-wali – or wala – grinning from ear to ear. I still have to guess and I still have to mark, but my brain doesn't want to work so hard any more. It just wants – as does the rest of me – more of the same treatment, any of the treatments so far, as long as I can take some matters into my own hands. But the time for that is not yet, and I wrench myself back from the sweet seep of wetness at my core to wonder if that was Neerja or Vini.

~

N and V are, as indicated earlier, a couple, currently practising monogamy-of-sorts. Nobody's quite sure *what* sort, just as nobody's sure which live-in or currently dating couples in our wider concentric circles are *not* monogamous. There's theory and there's practice, there are fierce discussions and there's many a slip (or non-slip, depending on how you look at it), but very few care to wear their monogamy, if any, on their sleeve, except for those in the outermost ripples who do so as a matter of course. I think of N and C as rather brave, for this reason. It's why tonight they're playing for fun and not for stakes. Mandira's not competing either, because of a frozen shoulder. I arrive at a decision.

'Vini. And, let's see – 7.25.'

'How wonderfully precise!'

'And how honest – considering that if your guess is right, Jo, you could have said "ten" and it would make no difference.'

'Well, if that *was* Vini then can you imagine the swollen head!'

'Or nose in the air . . .'

'Since you guys insist on talking about me like I'm not here, I may as well go get myself a plate of food.'

'Vini come back! All is forgiven!'

'Vini, come back with more ice! This has all melted.'

'Get your own ice, Hothead!'

I imagine Vini in her purple shirt and round glasses and wonder how she's doing, really. She's just come out to her parents, who are divorced, and her father's not talking to her, while the mother blames the father when she isn't blaming herself or weeping on the phone and demanding Vini come home to Vizag so she can talk to her 'properly'. They don't even know about the 'steady partner' bit yet; while Neerja does have, of all things, a supportive and evidently heterosexual twin brother who gets a lot of teasing sympathy from her friends for having missed out on the gay gene. And suddenly it hits me – oops! that nosing was such a dog-inspired thing, it must have been Neerja and not Vini. Neerja's actually a vet, and a sort of honourary dog herself. 'Can I change my guess?' I ask, but of course that's against the Rules.

~

We still have to work out the nitty-gritties, but if I have more right guesses than wrong, all the better for me, obviously. And now I need time out to pee. This involves being untied and escorted to the loo by Ruchi, unblinfolded just outside so that I don't see anyone or anything that might clue me in, and then getting the full regalia back on before we continue. A tad regretfully, I use the water spray thingy to rinse off the stickiness below as well, pat myself dry, then spend a long time looking at myself in the mirror and pulling faces and wondering should I use the mouthwash or will that muddy the waters. I settle for a splash of water on my flushed face and some wistful work with an earbud, before emerging in a quite virginal state, my senses and other things all nice and cool again.

Ruchi looks somewhat troubled, and I notice the door of the bedroom we're in is now shut. She tells me in low tones that we have an unexpected guest. Queer, and a good friend of Abhay's. He'd invited her because he's been wanting her to meet us, and then she said she couldn't make it, so when we began he didn't say anything, but apparently she got unexpectedly free and just landed up. Anyway the thing now is, would I like us to carry on? Or should we postpone the rest of it till next time? Knowing there's a stranger in our midst, my comfort level drops. I say that if she seems okay and if Abhay trusts her, she can be an observer; she needn't know anything more than that it's a party guessing game.

But no sooner does the new arrival see me than she exclaims, 'Jyotsna! Am I dreaming?' The deep voice is deeply familiar yet I cannot place it, and then my shoulders are gripped hard by the owner of the voice as Abhay says, astounded, 'You guys *know* each other?' Before I can frame an answer, I find myself being bear-hugged, and kissed on both cheeks.

'Looks like Romila is playing too,' Tanu observes dryly.

'Romila!' I squeal. 'Omigod where have *you* sprung from? I *knew* I knew that voice! People come on, untie me, I have to see her!' I'm granted this concession and there she is, Romi, my old college crush: the slim volleyball champ, now more comfortable around the midriff than before; her mass of below-the-shoulder curls replaced by a short stylish mop. We smile at each other amazed and I hold out my arms, closing with my return hug the fourteen-year gap. Finally I put into words my sense of grievance – 'But you were straight as an arrow! What happened?'

'A bad divorce happened, my dear, and then the best sex of my life – with a woman – and then Abhay.' When Tanu goes aaaah, Romi is quick to clarify, 'Oh, he's not – we're not lovers. I'm hardly his type.' Abhay protests, and she gives him a playful sock on the jaw. 'Abhay and I are best buddies. He's my guide to all things queer. We're colleagues, you know.' I stare at Abhay, still wide-eyed and wonderstruck, and he's grinning and grinning like he's just given both of us the most beautiful present, which of course he has.

~

Romi has already been told there's some sort of party game in progress; now she is filled in on the details because of course she has to play. No observer status allowed, in the changed circumstances. And she's, well, game. This time I choose a spot nearer the fan. It's been getting warmer as the evening progresses, helped no doubt by the rushes of blood induced in me from time to time. On again go the ties that bind, and we're back in business. As the blindfold is tested, I realise I was too focused on Romi to make use of the opportunity to sneak-peek at details that might have helped. We began with my looking everyone over intently, after which I was meant to rely on memory, not to mention the fine arts of deduction, intuition and wild guesswork.

This continues to be my modus operandi as Number Four is called.

Either they're getting better or I'm getting more and more turned on, or both. Inspired perhaps by the nose performance, this one's all hand job and then some. Soft as palms and pads, sharp as nails. S/he goes from slow and gentle strokes to swifter and rougher, and every cell of my cheeks and forehead and scalp and neck and throat comes alive; s/he bunches portions of my hair and pulls and lets go like a practised masseuse and then it's the outer ridges of my ears being raked in tandem by the nails; all of a sudden the fingers play fast and furious with my face, kneading it roughly, grabbing and jabbing at my flesh. Then with an unexpected return to tenderness palms cup my cheeks as lips descend to mine for a satisfying finish. We take a moment or three to break out of the liplock after time is called.

~

I lean my head back and allow myself a happy sigh. My body feels utterly relaxed and wholly aroused at the same time. I could go to sleep; I could go on for hours. But first I have to say my piece. It's too soon for Romi to get into the act, I think. Abhay? I don't know if Abhay would do that stuff with the nails. And Mandira doesn't have nails – she once told me how she always stops biting them when in a relationship and goes back to chewing them out of existence after a break-up: making it amusing; making it seem like being in and out of relationships continually is the natural order of things for her; completely glossing over the heartbreak. Not all the people in this room know that she has been in therapy for over a year, in and out of clinical depression, mainly.

'Wake up, Jo!'

'I'm awake. Wide awake. Just savouring it all.' Suddenly I'm convinced my last guess was wrong and that *this* must have been Vini. Not that I'm sure about any of my earlier guesses except for Tanu. I guess Vini again, and 6.75.

'Vini aka India's Most Wanted!'

'Jyotsna's Most Wanted, at any rate!'

'Maybe you'll get third time lucky, you two!' This last is obviously said to confuse and mislead. And I do wonder, how well am I guessing? Am I going to be rewarded, or punished?

'Will *anyone* score a perfect ten tod-ayyyy?' Mandira sings in operatic style.

'Or even eight-and-a-haaalf?' wonders Tanu.

'Let Number Fiiive tra-ayy the-ir luu-uck!' concludes Vini, hitting the high notes on 'Five' and slipsliding down an octave to an incredibly bass 'luck'.

~

Five snaps into it, and we're back to the convention of good old lips. But what a tantalising and evasive pair – gliding all over the place, all across my face, sometimes coming oh-so-close to my own lips then darting away to settle on nosebridge or temple, pressed together but lingering delectably, or apart with their hot wet soft insides all engaged, letting teeth graze and warm breath scorch my skin, running an exploratory tongue in maddening circles over my parched, arched throat. Playing catch-me-if-you-can, hovering again for two split seconds at the corner of my mouth, doing a licky-feely dash right across my upper lip. If only my hands were free and I could hold that head firmly in place and find its lips with mine, but that easy luxury is denied me so I twist and turn my own head trying to catch them in motion. At last they relent and meet me halfway; as I lean gratefully into the full-on kiss my entire face is on fire and the rest of me is gathered into a tight explosive ache just waiting to be touched off. Through the haze within and without I smell gin, I think, and a menthol cigarette. Abhay, 7.5.

'Oooh things are hotting up!'

'Highest so far.'

'How about a high-five, Number Five?' Palms are lightly clapped against each other, once, twice, thrice.

Abhay, if that's who it was, is a transman who's just recently back in circulation after his top surgery. His parents and sisters never had major issues with his gender identity but they balked at the idea of actual irreversible change, while his sexuality was never even up for discussion. Although they're supportive now, there was a period of estrangement after he left home with his then-girlfriend. Considering their running away from Jabalpur to Bombay was largely at the gf's instigation – to rescue her from the regular thrashings by her brother after he read an incriminatory email that she'd been careless enough to leave accessible – Abhay felt both insulted and injured when she left him five months later for what she called a 'real' man. He also saw the painfully black humour of being caught in what he refers to as 'such an unoriginal situation'. Today he wonders if it was an insecurity-fuelled self-fulfilling prophecy on his part, because she did precisely what he used to tell her she'd one day do. He wanted to hear her protest he was wrong, and protest she did, right up until the time she proved him right. Around the same time he quit the corporate job where they insisted on calling him Abha and where he couldn't figure whether it was more uncomfortable to have to use the women's loo, or the men's. Now he's with a new publishing venture that aims to bring out feminist and queer non-fiction, fiction – and poetry. I wonder if Romi's one of their editors.

According to my calculations there's Romi left, and Ruchi and Mandira – well, three people anyway – after which the two lowest scorers will have the option of a second chance.

~

What can I say about what follows except offer up thanks to human evolution which has led to such wondrous nerve-endings and to human creativity that works such wonders with them? Either this is somebody who's been here before, which narrows down the field, else I just got lucky. Whose mouth is this I do not know, pleasuring my right ear; whose hand caresses the back of my neck and moves to give my other ear a foretaste of things to come? This for me is erogenous terrain all the way; I am dissolving and my juices are in full flow as mouth and hand change sides and ears, sucking darting teasing biting, burrowing deep and delicious. I can no longer hold back the sounds of mounting bliss, I feel I'm about to come, I cry out inside – don't stop please! But of course it has to end and I'm left wet and shaken and breathless and yearning as time is called; exquisitely a forearm accidentally-on-purpose comes to rest on my breasts at the last moment, surreptitiously and briefly greeting my achingly hard nipples while a tongue still flickers rapidly inside my ear – a spot of cheating there, but I'm hardly going to be the one to point it out.

Silence. I probably have a silly smile plastered on my face but what the hell. It ended too soon and I can no longer separate torture from pleasure, delight from a kind of childish resentment.

Hoping hard this wasn't one of the three non-competitors, my voice is ragged as I manage to utter, 'Ten, that was a ten!' The silence eerily continues for two more beats, then there's a smattering of applause, surprisingly thin. And then Tanu's voice, 'Hang on, Jo, sorry. Guys, Mandira just had a call, her sister's taken a turn for the worse. She has to leave asap for Cal.' Oh no. Mandira's sister has lung cancer. A non-smoker, married to a heavy smoker who quit the day she was diagnosed. It was already fairly advanced and there's never been much hope, but this is sudden. When is it not, even when it's not? Tanu removes my bonds, and I see there's only Romi and Vini in the room besides her. After a while the others troop back in from the other room. Mandira, red-eyed, smiles at me bravely.

'You heard?' I nod, open my arms and give her a tight wordless hug. She sobs once, then collects herself. Everyone gathers around her, comforting, concerned.

'Jo gave the last one ten, Mandira!' Mandira smiles wanly. 'Oh damn! We missed the action.'

'And who did she guess?' Neerja wonders.

'Still waiting for that, but now she knows who was still in the room.'

'We can go into all that later . . . You better get going, sweetie,' I tell Mandira.

Ruchi and Neerja decide to accompany Mandira. There isn't any flight tonight, but they'll stay over at her place and see her off early morning. The three of them leave and we sit on soberly, sad and connected, speaking of cancer, sharing Mandira's imminent grief and recalling our own, older perhaps, yet tangible still. Then we have a last small drink each, serve ourselves some food, and Vini says, 'Okay, that last one – who do you think?' I'm totally at sea, but I guess Romi.

'It was Hothead!' says Vini, and I am nothing less than stunned.

'Then who . . . how . . . wow!'

'Oh, she dashed into the bedroom as soon as I called time. She must have realised something was up with half the people having disappeared in there, and also wanted to fool you maybe.'

And now it turns out that Number One was Mandira, not Bins – Mandira wasn't drinking, true, but she'd deviously run an ice cube over her lips. Two was Tanu, sure enough – nobody wore a wig to try and confuse me. Three *was* Vini, as I guessed, and not Neerja as I later thought – but when I tell them my reasoning about the nose, Vini laughs and says, 'Well, who do you think I acquired that special skill from?!' Four, right after the break and Romi's grand entry, actually *was* Romi, so I got that wrong too but I'm delighted she was so quick off the mark, that finally after all these years I got to kiss her, and that maybe we'll make up for lost time yet. Five was Benaifer, though I guessed Abhay, since I'd already guessed Bins at the start. So Abhay and Ruchi were the only ones left when the game broke up.

'But wait! You don't smoke, Bins, and I got this definite menthol ciggie whiff – that's why I said Abhay.'

'Yep, she took a couple of drags from me just before. You didn't think we were going to make it that easy for you?' Abhay laughs.

'Anyway I'm glad I scored 7.5 and not four,' says Bins, and it dawns on us that she's the winner, given that Number Six, Neerja of recent 'ten' fame, was a non-competitor.

'So Bins wins,' says Tanu. 'Congratulations, you lucky, lucky person.' For a moment I think Tanu means I am the lucky person, and I'm all set to agree, but then I see she's addressing Bins – I'm supposed to be the prize, after all.

Tanu and Bins have had an on-again-off-again thing for ages; recently Bins and Abhay have been spending time together but nobody knows what's up and it doesn't matter. They'll talk about it if and when they want to or need to. Not that sweeping assumptions have not been made, or indiscreet probing questions not asked – and pointedly ignored.

I turn to Benaifer, who says, 'Well, I win by default because two punters didn't get their turns, but I'm not going to be over-scrupulous and refuse my reward. Only thing is – Jo? I'm absolutely thrilled and delighted but can I take a rain check? After this whole Mandira thing, one's a bit low, yaar.'

'Yes, of course, I feel the same way – and there is, as we know, much pleasure in waiting!'

'Oh, I hope it won't be a long wait – I'll call you tomorrow and we'll fix a date.'

'Terrific.'

'And I still get to take you home. I'll drop you and carry on, how's that?'

'Perfect,' I say, 'and maybe we can get to know each other better on the way. Do it right and all.' Everybody laughs, because we all know each other pretty well already, except for Romi who soon will be one of the gang I hope.

~

We try to recall what rules we'd invented for right and wrong identification. Everyone's a bit fuzzy but we decide that I get a date each with the two top scorers from the accurate guess list. So I have not just Benaifer to look forward to, but hot sex with Tanu and a fun evening with Vini as well. My cup pretty much runneth over. Figuring out apt punishment for wrong guesses is left to some other time.

And then it's past two in the morning and everyone has to be at work in a few hours, so we say our goodbyes to Vini – which process takes another half hour. Abhay, Benaifer and Romi squabble briefly over what they call 'doing the honours'. Romi uses the 'oldest friend' line. Abhay, deliberately provocative, says he's the man and this is man's work, and gets called a few choice names. Tanu looks on amused, saying, 'I think Jo can manage quite well without any of you idiots.' And then Bins, tonight's winner, wordlessly wins the argument hands down: she simply grasps my chair from behind and wheels me out towards the lift.

The Half Day

Doabi

Mannat walked into her apartment, dropped her bags to the floor, kicked off her shoes and pushed her dishevelled hair off her face. It was Saturday, her favourite day, her half day, her day of solace. Without exception, her Saturday after-work routine consisted of switching off her mobile, shopping for provisions after work, changing into her favourite worn-out salwar and t-shirt, making her favourite meal, taking a long, hot shower, eating while reading the latest trashy novel and drinking a glass of beer or wine depending on the meal, her mood and the weather. Saturday night could turn into anything else, but after work it was her time.

Winter was ending in Delhi and that meant that the sun was finally showing its face, streaming into her immaculate kitchen. Mannat rolled up the sleeves of her shirt, so that she could absorb the warmth before it gave itself over to the chilly evening. For a brief moment, she closed her eyes and imagined that she could perform photosynthesis to replenish the energy that the cold winter took away from her. She switched on her favourite Rafi CD and felt the weariness of the week fade as she peered into the bowl of soaking rajma.

The rajma had plumped up and some of the beans were splitting. They were a deep maroon. These ones were special because she had carefully carried them back to the city from her father's farm; in that moment, each grain was more precious to her than her entire book collection. She roughly chopped the tomatoes, peeled the onion, ginger, garlic and threw them into the mixie with the chillies. She switched on the gas, let its flame heat the vessel and put a conservative amount of oil into it. Now came her favourite part: she cautiously dropped one jeera seed into the oil, and it immediately floated to the top, making a satisfying crackle. The time had come – she threw a handful of the jeera into the oil and followed up with the tadka: the tomato, onion, ginger, garlic, chilli mixture. The smells of the frying tadka were so pleasing that she smiled on the outside. When the tadka turned burgundy, the oil separated from it; she threw everything else in then and put the lid on the pressure cooker.

As the steam built inside the pressure cooker, Mannat washed the dhania and chopped it finely. She thought about the contrast of the fresh green dhania on the deep red rajma and felt her belly rumble. She sliced a small onion into fine strips to eat on the side and threw it into water to take away the sharpness. She washed the rice and threw in a few spices to magnify the already fragrant basmati. Now that her dinner was at the stage of preparing itself, she could think about the next stage of her half-day ritual. As Mannat went to switch on the geyser for her pre-dinner bath, she remembered that she had forgotten to set the dahi this morning. She could not eat rajma chawal without dahi; it would not do the rajma justice. She'd just have to make do with bazaari dahi. After the last whistle of pressure cooker, she grudgingly picked up her chunni, threw it over her t-shirt, and resentfully headed out towards the provisions store around the corner.

'Mannat! Mannat! Hi!' she heard someone call after her. Reluctantly, she turned around and saw a perky, over-kajaled woman approaching her.

'Oh, hi,' she said, inquisitively at first. 'Hi. Hi, sorry I didn't recognise you . . . er, I mean you look different in the day. I . . . I'm sorry, you know what I mean? It's Sundeep, right?'

'Actually, my name is Manpreet.'

For Mannat, a one-night stand was usually about satisfying her own sexual desires without the complication of caring. She usually didn't follow up or even give a second thought after the person left her apartment.

After a moment of tension, 'Sorry,' Mannat said, a little indifferently.

'Oh, it's ok. Just thought that I would say hello. Anyway, I'm just on my way to meet a friend. See you around.' Manpreet awkwardly shuffled her feet. She gave Mannat a smile and walked off in the opposite direction.

~

All evening, even though the rajma turned out superbly and her favourite songs came on the radio while she showered,

Mannat couldn't shake the feeling that she had been incredibly rude to Manpreet. She kept trying to think of nicer ways to say what she had said to her.

Mannat lay down on her sofa and cracked open her brand-new Zadie Smith novel and pushed the encounter on the street out of her mind. The next thing she knew, she had read 75 pages and drunk half a bottle of Sula Mosaic. Just as she readjusted her position, the doorbell rang. She glanced at the clock: 11.45 p.m. There was only person who would knowingly interrupt her half-day ritual.

'Hey faggot!' Mannat exclaimed as she unlatched the door. 'Oh ... shit ... hi ... Manpreet, what are you doing here? Sorry, I thought you were someone else.'

'You are a bitch with the worst one-night-stand etiquette, you know that?'

'You're drunk, but I take your criticism. Come in and abuse me, I don't want to create a scene for the neighbours.'

Manpreet stumbled into the door, trying to maintain her composure.

'Would you like a drink of water or wine?' asked Mannat politely.

'Wine.'

'Wine, it is. Listen, I'm sorry about how I said what I said. You are right, that wasn't cool.' Mannat handed Manpreet a glass of wine as she apologised.

'Yeah, you were a total bitch ... unfortunately, bitches get me wet.'

'Oh lord, now are you going to go all psycho on me? Showing up drunk at my house, creating a scene and then hitting on me? Listen, I really don't want any drama.'

'I just want a fuck, actually. But that's ok, see you around.' Manpreet put her hand on the doorknob.

'Wait . . . wait a second,' Mannat slid treacherously close to her. 'You should at least finish your drink.' Manpreet took a big swig from her glass and wiped her mouth. She raised one eyebrow at Mannat.

Mannat slinked even closer to Manpreet. The electricity was palpable. Manpreet could feel her breath on her neck. Mannat pounced on her and pushed her against the door. They were nose to nose. With danger in her voice, Mannat whispered, 'Don't make me regret this.' Manpreet struggled to kiss her, but was pinned down and overpowered. Mannat pressed up against her and devoured her neck. 'Listen to me carefully, ok? I am going to fuck you silly very slowly, ok?' she breathed into her ear.

As she began to stroke Manpreet's breasts, Manpreet grabbed her breasts in turn. She swiftly found her hands swatted. 'I think that you didn't hear me. I am going to fuck YOU silly. Nowhere in that sentence is there anything about you being allowed to touch me.' Manpreet looked at her with desperation. 'Please,' she pleaded. Mannat leaned down to sweetly kiss Manpreet's cheek, just to tease her. She started feeling her breasts again through the kurta, pinching her nipples and then squeezing her breasts while nibbling on her neck. She continued to nibble and suck her neck, her jawbone and behind her ears. When she started licking the outside of the ear, that resulted in low moans; Mannat was very pleased with herself. She put her hands inside the kurta and unclasped Manpreet's bra. Her breasts were now free. She took Manpreet's nipples between her thumb and fingers and rolled them until they were rigid, pleased at the effect under the translucent white fabric. She continued kissing behind Manpreet's ears, feeling the tension rising from pleasure to frustration. She took Manpreet's kurta off completely and started kissing around her nipples, until she finally took a nipple and pushed it into her mouth. She greedily sucked on it, teasing the tip with her tongue while preparing the other one with her hand.

Manpreet had been running her hand through Mannat's hair. Growing impatient, she started gently pushing Mannat's head a little, just to give her an indication of what she wanted. Mannat kissed her way back up, murmuring 'Suggestion duly noted, but I'm not really looking for your input.' She started hungrily kissing her mouth again, going from lips to neck to ear with increased force. She started kissing down again, kissing Manpreet's round belly, her sides. With a mischievous look, she reached for the chunni she'd worn over her t-shirt. She took Manpreet's hands and tied them up in front of her, then continued to kiss her belly along the top of her jeans. The smell of Manpreet's wetness made her grin.

Mannat undid the button on the jeans and slid them and the underwear off. Kneeling on the floor, she kissed the inside of Manpreet's thigh. 'Ok, now I want you to flip over and lean against the arm of the sofa with your bum facing me.' Manpreet's eyes widened at the prospect of being in such a vulnerable position. Yet her face betrayed her; the idea of being put in this submissive position made her feel even more naked and horny than before. Mannat started running her fingers from the top of Manpreet's neck down to the base of her spine. As her fingers drifted further down, she could feel the other woman's body overwrought with excitement verging on discomfort. She grazed the inside of her buttocks, producing shivers. Manpreet writhed in a pleasure that could only be felt for a fraction of a second – any longer would have resulted in a small death. Mannat knew that fine line, as well as the one between pleasure and pain. On the edge of the moment of pleasure, she smacked Manpreet's ass and then immediately kissed it. She gently rubbed her hands along the bottom of her ass, just grazing her vagina. Much to her delight, she saw that this stimulus had made Manpreet's pussy start to drip. Mannat touched the droplet of moisture and let it fall onto her finger. She revelled in the power of being able to produce such bodily reactions in a woman. Catching Manpreet's eye, she raised one eyebrow like Rekha in *Umrao Jaan*. Slowly lifting her finger with Manpreet's secretions to her lips, she licked it clean.

'Come to bed. Lie on your back. You can put your hands on your belly,' she commanded.

On the bed, she sat between Manpreet's thighs, gazing at her vagina for a brief second. Mannat shimmied out of her salwar and underwear and mounted Manpreet in the scissors position. They were vagina to vagina. Their clits met, their wetness mingled, they fit together so perfectly that they should have been on a gay-rights poster just to show people exactly how natural gay sex is. She started riding Manpreet in a slow, steady rhythm. Mannat rubbed her swollen clit against Manpreet's. As she did this, she became even more engorged; she started fucking Manpreet with her clit. Faster and faster, with more pressure; they were both moaning with pleasure and staring at each other with incredulity at the sheer hotness of the act. Just as they were both about to climax, Mannat slid off. She wasn't going to let anyone get off that easily.

She moved up to Manpreet's mouth, hovering there just long enough to give her a single taste. Then Mannat moved back down with her head between Manpreet's thighs. This time she just went for it. She started licking Manpreet's clit with a voracious appetite and plunged her fingers straight into her vagina. She was licking with fast flicks of her tongue and fucking with deep thrusts, wanting to be as far inside of her as possible. With her free hand, she started fingering her ass, placing her knees on her shoulders, so that she could get more leverage. She had Manpreet's clit in her mouth, two fingers in her vagina and one in her ass. They were both in sheer corporeal bliss. Mannat glanced up and saw that Manpreet's face was begging her to slow down. She incrementally geared down to long, hard, deep, slow thrusts and the lightest of flicks with her tongue. She took the finger out of the ass and started paying Manpreet's clit the attention that it deserved, all the while fucking her unhurriedly. She sucked her clit and released then licked. Suck, release, lick, suck, release, lick, suck, release, lick. Manpreet could feel Mannat on the edge of a 7.8-on-the-Richter-scale orgasm. She started to rub Manpreet's clit with her thumb with fast, deliberate motions.

'OH FUCK!' Manpreet came like an earthquake. 'STOP! I can't take anymore. Please stop.' Manpreet tried to push her hands out.

Mannat gave her a mischievous look. Very, very slowly, she started to take her fingers out of Manpreet; every millimetre that she took out made Manpreet gasp with pleasure. When Mannat finally took her fingers out, they were dripping wet. She kissed her vagina once more and popped her fingers slick with Manpreet into her mouth. She slurped and savoured the juice on her fingers like it was the dregs of jal jeera after a round of gol guppe.

'Well, that was fun,' Mannat said lightly as she rolled out of bed.

'Can you give me a couple minutes to recover?' Manpreet asked meekly.

'Sure, take your time. I'll be on the couch reading Zadie. The bathroom is on your right, if you want to wash your face or something.'

~

Manpreet walked into the living room to find Mannat lounging on the couch. 'I should get going,' she declared.

'Listen, you should sober up before you head out.' Mannat handed her a piping hot bowl of rajma chawal, the white rice peeking out under the deep dark red beans garnished with green cilantro, the translucent purple onions on the side.

'Do you have any dahi?'

'Of course, let me get it for you.'

After Manpreet polished off the meal, she said, 'I don't know what was better, the orgasm or that bowl.'

Mannat opened the door, smiled and said, 'If we run into each other again, be sure to say hello.'

RAJMA CHAWAL THE PUNJABI WAY

INGREDIENTS:

For the Rajma:

- One ½ cup kidney beans (rajma)
- One tablespoon salt (adjust to taste)
- Two large tomatoes (tamatar)
- One tablespoon ginger (adrak)
- One tablespoon garlic (lasoon)
- 1-4 green chillies (hari mirch)
- Three tablespoon oil
- One tablespoon cumin seeds (jeera)
- ½ teaspoon turmeric (haldi)
- ½ teaspoon red chilli powder (adjust to taste)
- 1/2 teaspoon black pepper

Garnish and on the side

- One medium sliced onion for eating on the side
- Sprinkle of roasted ground cumin (jeera powder)
- A handful of coriander (dhania) for garnish
- ½ lime, squeezed
- Curd on the side

Rice:

- Two cups basmati rice
- Two cups water

- Two bay leaves (tej patta)
- Two cloves (long)
- One black cardamom (kali elaichi)

METHOD:

1. Wash and soak the kidney beans in about six cups of water for at least six hours, though overnight is best (kidney beans will double in volume after soaking).

2. Cut the tomatoes in small pieces, slice the green chilli(es) lengthwise and take out the seeds (if you prefer mild). Next, in the mixie, blend the tomatoes, green chilli(es), garlic and ginger to make a paste.

3. Slice the onion into thin strips and immerse in cold water.

4. Heat the oil in pressure cooker. Test the heat by adding one cumin seed. If the seed rises to the top and crackles right away, the oil is ready. Add cumin seeds. As the cumin seeds crackle, add the tomato, chilli, garlic, ginger paste, turmeric, chilli powder, and black pepper.

5. Fry until the mixture is burgundy in colour and the oil separates from the mixture.

6. Add the kidney beans, salt, and three cups of water. Close the cooker. Cook on medium-high heat.

7. As the pressure cooker starts steaming, turn the heat down to medium and cook for about seven whistles.

8. Wash the basmati rice until the water runs clear. Crush the black cardamom. In a wide pot, put in the rice, water and all the spices. Simmer on medium heat until water is absorbed.

9. Turn off the heat and wait until steam has escaped on its own before opening the pressure cooker.

10. The kidney beans should be soft and tender. Adjust salt and pepper to your taste.

11. Garnish with coriander.

12. Remove sliced onions from water. Squeeze lime over them and mix with salt and roasted powdered cumin.

13. Serve the kidney beans on basmati rice with curd and onions on the side.

14. Enjoy!

Upstairs, Downstairs

Nikhil Yadav

I keyed in the piece my editor wanted and hurried down the building to take an autorickshaw from the crowded ITO intersection. Stepping out onto the road, I saw the busy crowds, buses, autorickshaws and street-vendors blurred by the invisible heat released by the tarmac, slow cooking everyone on the ITO intersection into an indistinguishable human stew.

Daily work on the city beat in my newspaper had become one of those things where you twiddled your pencil the whole day and, when you hadn't come up with anything by six o'clock, you keyed in the story that the editor wanted in thirty minutes flat. Somewhere in the inner columns (if you cared enough for that in the rushed mornings), reeling under the weight of celebrity photo-ops, Sudoku, movie listings and homeopathic advice, you might find a column on the mouldy bylanes and crumbling ruins of a Delhi hidden from someone like yourself. That piece is written by me. A fresh-off-the-boat migrant helping the English-reading dilliwallahs see their city from a foreign perspective. My personal mission of creating an alternative niche in a mainstream daily and telling people about the Delhi hidden from all of us, I was beginning to understand, was a double-edged sword. It gets you recognition, but like a noose steadily tightening around your neck, your range gets narrower by the day. The stories had already begun to thin and the beat, I felt, was getting repetitive.

There's a reason why dailies, such as the one I work for, are able to pay not-too-bad salaries to me and my ilk, and that reason is advertising. The earlier I understood that, the better for me. I needed to repeat these things to myself on evenings like today when I left the office with little more than a mild sense of having betrayed myself.

~

Dusk was settling in over Delhi as the autorickshaw battled its way through evening traffic and lurched past Pragati Maidan, Tilak Marg, India Gate and the merry-go-around of Lutyens Delhi. The auto would stop at a red light and eyes would try to seek out that guilty look, that sideways glance, that forthright stare, all part of a signature handshake that strangers gave each other before the light turned green and everyone went their own way. All along the shadowlands of the city's railway lines, parks and public toilets, a penumbral existence was beginning to wiggle its way out. Eyes lingering in curiosity, darting about seeking recognition for a common ache, and the quick second that passes between recognition and action. Where daily boredom can end in a flash with mouths gorging at crotches, with hands rubbing warmth into cocks gone flaccid by sitting too long behind desks. Where this evening, lady luck could bring for you the thousand indignities your brain has been feverishly fantasizing about all day long. Everything popping out joyously in this pasture of the fearful, empty, twilight spaces of the city. As we passed by the Pragati Maidan intersection I remembered the long empty lane behind the railway colony where, in a dark corner a footballer had dropped his loose shorts and, with my arms around his footballers' legs, I had senselessly eaten what had been offered so generously. A quiet celebration of accidental sex right there in the unlit lanes of a railway colony, to the dismal sounds of pressure-cookers going off in kitchens and housewives settling in front of their television sets and the trains roaring past behind us, sending shivers all across our bodies. Well, there was no room for such hunting today, so we sped on.

~

I had never met Binoo Nanda, but I expected her to be one of the Khan Market women sporting kohl, Bhagalpur silk, heirloom pearls and a favourite cause. Binoo had of late converted her basement into a free performance venue and today, a fledgling experimental group was slated to perform two solos. There was a very correct sounding fund-raiser sideshow, which had also been mentioned in the invite, but I'd forgotten exactly what it was.

I reached predictably late and entered a house in one of those plush South Delhi colonies where the only people you ever actually see on the road are the servants and the night-watch guards. Stepping inside one of these mansions, I was greeted by silence, perhaps the first and most powerful ingredient of the luxury that the rich enjoy. My shoes creaked as I entered this realm, my clothes rustled and I could even hear the rude crackling of my joints. Clambering down to the basement, I was ushered into a waiting room. The first solo had already begun and I was told I would only be able to enter at the beginning of the second act.

~

In the middle of the performance I wanted to stand up and scream – who gave the right to these young twats to talk about such things? I looked around indignantly to see signs of anyone else reacting in the same way. There were two guys in the middle, gay and foreigners both, wrapped in muscle tees and keffiyeh, humming and lip-syncing to the tunes that the silly girl on the stage was playing on a tape-recorder. We're getting all the cultural references, aren't we? But looking a bit longer, I saw there was something more to their nonchalance than plain snobbery and I realized that they were really trying to overcome the embarrassment of sitting amongst a group of people all of whom had suddenly gone quiet. Come to think of it, it was a bit eerie. I could hear some sniffling in some corner and maybe, or did I just imagine it, a stifled sob. An elderly couple got up and left in the middle of the performance. The silly girl on the stage, she must just be out of college, stayed in her role throughout. With a concern that she had never felt for anything in her own life yet, she went on talking about a dead friend, about his sudden death from some very rare disease, then moving on to philosophize about the death of the young, about death which is quick and painless, about the apathy of the world, and so on. It was all profound in an adolescent sort of way, inexperience masquerading in an excess of feeling. The young, I chuckled. Death is just an abstraction for attention when you're young. Do you really believe we'll mistake it for sensitivity? You deserve to be slapped for talking about things you do not understand. The brochure told us the girl had written the piece herself. Just shut up and get laid lady, I wanted to shout.

The real drama, though, was unfolding on the side of the audience. A loose cannon had gone off in our midst and I saw that some in the audience were holding on to the legs of their chairs to keep their composure. All the while the two gay men kept on humming, continuing to appreciate the choice of songs. The girl went on singing, humming, choking and hamming about death, bereavement, mortality, memory. Shit, shit, shit! I found myself dropping my face in my hands and shaking my head, unable to believe in the misplaced confidence of those who know they will be heard.

Having reached the conclusion of the ostensibly intense meditation, the solo act wound up just as it had begun, abruptly. There was some hasty applause after which the hostess got up to address us all. Binoo Nanda was a sharp woman. She'd realized that the debut of her Downstairs arena had turned into a downright disaster. She thanked the performer somewhat hurriedly and then launched into a long, moving apology. She confessed she hadn't known the play would have such a theme, so disturbing to some present. Then she went on personally to acknowledge and apologize to as many as seven families sitting there. It seems that all of them had lost a young son. Someone's son had been reported missing on a trekking trip; another washed away in an undertow; someone else in a car accident; another to a congenital disorder. She mentioned the couple who had left in the middle had lost a son too. My shock was unspeakable. I couldn't understand how, in an audience not exceeding fifty people, so many of them shared similar tragedies. I couldn't understand why Binoo Nanda kept on narrating instances of the death of young men. Did the rich grieve more about their young men like some warrior tribes are known to do or had they not mourned enough? Maybe it was one of those mythical curses that we hear of in epics that continue over several generations. Meanwhile Binoo leaned over and lovingly hugged a woman in the second row. She had managed to say just the right things and everyone seemed palpably relieved after her speech.

She moved on to talk about the fund-raising aspect of the evening. Things became considerably more cheerful after that. It was as if Binoo's speech was the unwritten final act of a drama without which the audience would have been left shattered and disconsolate. Everyone was feeling much better and the awkwardness over tragedies, real and staged, had been washed away by Binoo's bravura performance. We all moved towards beer and food. I felt pretty messed up by all this. It was almost as if I had just witnessed a nerve-wracking road accident which miraculously turned out to be pleasant for all involved. I dashed more eagerly than anybody else towards the bar.

~

The small gathering began to break into groups. No phone signal in the basement, so people had begun to walk up and out into the driveway and the patio. There was a group of youngsters sharing a smoke in the driveway. I could see their smoke huddle from the ventilator of the basement room. I tried to look around for a familiar face to gravitate towards but there was none. I wasn't old and rich, I didn't smoke and I had nobody but myself to blame for my asocial grumpiness. The few who were left around me were all middle-aged and in a moment of utter boredom I let out a voluble sigh, leaned my back against the wall, folded my right leg against it and tugged at my beer in what looked like a parody of the bored gay man striking a desperate gigolo pose after a night of futile dancing when all the moves have yielded no return.

A middle-aged man in a paisley shirt was sitting with a group of women on a cushion on the floor. He was massaging the feet of one who looked exactly like Binoo. My reckless staring and insolent pose must have made the group self-conscious and he turned and spoke, 'Well, young man, don't just stand there, go ahead and enjoy yourself. Have they put the dinner out?' I shrugged in response.

Binoo, who must have been around, joined the group and took the sting out of the awkwardness by introducing me. The man was a Professor of History at a university close by, one of the women was Binoo's own twin sister (that explained the similarity) and the other was another Mrs Singh who was on the advising committee of some foundation for promotion of the arts. She too had more than a fleeting resemblance to Binoo. I made the ultimate blunder of asking if even she was related to Binoo.

'Of course not, whatever would make you think we were?' they all guffawed.

Well, I wanted to answer, that's because you all look and behave exactly as if you were one big blood-clan, you wear similar clothes, you talk of the same things, know everything about each other, and agree on most things. And although your main concern, like everybody else's, is property and money, you have enough style to actually begin your conversations with it. Even your teeth are the same tint of white, all of you smile and hug a lot. It's almost as if you *wanted* to have the same set of features, and through generations of pedigreed inbreeding you have actually succeeded in creating just that: a different race of the rich.

Binoo picked up the mantle of politeness from where I had dropped it and gave a glowing introduction. While our hostess was being her pleasant best, I felt a stare from the crowd around the staircase (was it towards me?) but I was a bit lightheaded and frankly didn't care enough.

The Professor was the first to pick up on repairing the conversation, 'Ah! So you are the Shashank who regales us with stories of the forgotten ruins and quarters of Delhi? I must admit I have a special interest in your stories.'

'You know, though Prodeep is a mediaeval Delhi specialist, I don't know anybody who knows our Delhi of today more than him. I use his academic specialisation to get directions when I'm lost and my driver can't find the address and he's never failed me. Not once. Prodeep, you remember the time when I had to go to the pushta for flood-relief, it was as far out as I had ever been and . . .'

'Well, that's because I know more about the bowels and the armpits of the city than its monuments, Binoo. My research, you'll excuse me, is on the sewers and gutters of Delhi and not on its ruins.'

'You should have been born in Paris dear, or at least some of those Middle-Eastern cities with great civic consciousness. What sewers? We have shit flying all around us!' Everyone laughed.

A young guy walked up and spoke to Mrs Singh. 'So how long you think you're gonna be here? 'Coz I think I'm gonna split soon. You want me to call for your car?'

'Sure dear, carry on . . . I'm having such a relaxed time for once. A nice play by talented young people and an evening with friends. Binoo, what a fantastic idea. Great work!' squealed Mrs Singh.

'Talking of talented people, have you met Shashank? He's one of our bright sparks in journalism. I'm hoping he will write good things about our Downstairs,' added Binoo. She was the only one I knew who could let drop the mask of conviviality, reveal her true intentions and still continue to be polite. But my concern had already shifted to the new subject who'd walked in on us, and in accordance with years of training as a gay man I sized him up in less time than it takes to say hello. Broad shoulders, somewhat stockily set, can't be more than late twenties despite the receding hairline, more than a grizzle on the chin and preppy clothes, very Ivy League! He gave an interested handshake, looked me straight in the eyes and said, 'Hi! Jayant.'

'So, I'll be going. See you in the morning, mom. See you,

Binoo.' He was leaning over and kissing Binoo when in a flash, I realized that this was my opportunity. If nothing else, I'd get out of this fiendish basement where they trap unsuspecting souls and torture them with culture.

'Binoo, I'd better be leaving too, long distance to go.'

'Oh!'

'Yeah, yeah . . . look I've picked up the brochures. I'll get back to you when I've done the piece. What with the editorial page layout and things . . . expect it in three days? I'll let you know.'

Ivy League had gone back to a group of people, saying his byes to them. There! there was that turned glance again. I moved into the corner of the room and towards the drinks table under the staircase. The steps of the staircase had formed a nice alcove. It was a perfect corner for lingering and deliberating some delay tactics without being seen by Binoo and the other denizens of her dreary Downstairs. I grabbed another pint and stood in the gigolo pose. Nothing leads to sex more directly than an affected pose of boredom. This time I had some hope for the right message to be relayed. Ivy League came right over.

'One for the road? Not a bad idea.'

'Yeah, I want the buzz to last till I crash on my bed. Can't really look forward to anything else from tonight, can I? And who knows, maybe I'll die of some rare disease in the back of an autorickshaw. They may make a play about it then.'

'Yeah . . . It was an interesting play.' Barely a chuckle.

I realised I was getting ahead of myself. Maybe he had

friends in the repertory. He was playing it safe with his opinions (if he had any) but in the partial secrecy of the alcove he was being daring enough to let his glance skim over my arms for just a bit. A little workout bump gleamed from under the arm-hugging tee I was wearing. In the distance, History Professor was using his lecturing voice with a pretty young thing. God! She must be younger than his students.

'I always tell my students that the idea of decadent young Mughal princes is a myth based out of social envy. Do you think its possible to have a continuous dynastic rule over, well, something over three hundred years, if everyone was busy having orgies and reading poetry? We have to understand the complex social psychology of inheritance to really understand what a life of privilege entailed for an *umrao* or a Mughal prince . . .' And so on.

'So where do you get back to?' a voice much closer enquired, bringing me back to attention. The beer was making me distracted.

'Oh! The back of the beyond. I have to cross a river and reach a corner of Delhi where the South Delhi imagination cannot go.' I wanted to check my bitchiness but I knew I was taking out my disgust about the evening and also about something else. 'Social envy' was it? But this guy was the most interesting thing happening out of this morbid evening and he was willing to drop me off at a distance. This was no time for introspection.

The rest happened unexpectedly smoothly. We got out together after finishing the beers, got into his blue-grey

Endeavour and drove off to the sound of classic rock. We talked idly, he pulled the car over to roll a joint, we drove on. Something was not quite right. The telltale signs of sexual interest apart, just about everything about this guy was so straight. The talk banal, not a sliver of excitement about it. He must have played some sport in college but the thickening midriff spoke of neglect. He was beginning to get typically squat and stocky. The grizzle on the face was an attempt to cover a doubling chin and to compensate for a receding hairline. In terms of a gay man closing in on thirty, this was, of course, a condition worse than death. A moment when you embraced your mortality and adopted a dog. But this guy oozed an unruffled, solid masculinity and it was impossible to visualize him in a gay club or among any of the other pheromonal performances of gay life. And yet I had undoubtedly been picked up with the effortless assurance of somebody who knew the drill like a routine. This must be how the rich, public-school type pick up boys, I speculated as Bruce Springsteen sang *I'm on fire* on the stereo. From their own surroundings, rather than in gay clubs. The world must be just a normal extension of their boarding schools where they know that men will always get it on with other men.

We drove into the gated, heavily guarded insides of a New Friends Colony block and the hush of the rich descended around us. I could hear the loud rustle of tree branches swaying a paean to solid property and wealth.

'And here we are. This is my mother's house or what I call our very own Liberace mansion.'

'I can see that.' I stood gawking at the Hussain horse that was eight inches away from your face as soon as you entered. Looking around, I saw it was true. There they were, the Queen Anne style sofas, Georgian cabinets piled with coffee-table books, gilded candelabras, Chinese screens, Wedgewood plates, sink in carpets and rococo mirrors pressing down upon you from everywhere. Walking in, I saw in one corner a sepia picture of his parents in a friendly pose with a very young Indira Gandhi in that cold, stunning look she had with sunglasses on.

The modern Indian masters followed us as we climbed up the staircase, the souzas, swaminathans and gujrals. Halting with a fumbling of keys on the second floor. 'Who stays on the first?' I asked. 'Well, nobody currently. It was meant for my elder brother but he is no longer with us,' he replied matter-of-factly.

The chill of the evening's performance entered my heart again. On that landing on the second floor in that desolate staircase I felt I was entering a cursed territory. With someone who is the sole survivor, the seed and sustenance of one of the cursed clans of the young dead.

Inside his apartment I settled into a comfortable chaise lounge whereas Ivy League went to get some more beer. His own place, like everything else about the guy, was indifferently arranged. There was a large TV set hung up on the wall and some massive sound system surrounding it. There was the usual bric-a-brac, a college photograph with a girl in it. On the wall opposite me there hung a painting of two naked women. One was a light skinned, small-breasted, taut, muscular girl standing, her arm slung consolingly over the other, dark-skinned, sumptuous, sitting swathed in a white sheet. The white of the sheet seemed to sear through the painting like a flame. I drew my breath in and almost whistled. Was that what I thought it was?

'Is that an Amrita Shergill?!'

'Yeah yeah. My mom is related to the father's side of her family. It's been with us for ages.'

Here we go, the family tree answer. It was impossible to enter into a conversation with this guy and not have some part of the great network of family and connections being thrown at you. He came straight over and plunked the beer on the table and immediately started necking me. I picked up the beer while he was doing that and gulped some down. Till that final second there was a little voice in my head uncertain of where I was and what I was doing there. The suspense was finally over. Without being strict about definitions, an accredited heterosexual man had definitely picked me up and we were open for business.

Within minutes of shirtless groping and biting – and I must admit I was getting increasingly amazed at the expertise with which this guy manoeuvered his way – I found myself being led into the bedroom. We threw ourselves down into inebriated digging into each other's bodies. I've mostly been drawn to the sleek, bony, barely-twenty type of guy, so his smooth mass of girth was a bit of a novelty for me. I hung on to the substance of his folds as he repeatedly worked his hands, mouth and tongue over me. The night's drinking, the strangeness of the evening and this even stranger encounter had begun to hit my head. The steady base of reality was fast slipping as panic-stricken jolts of ecstasy took over. Soon, his body lost its intactness and became something fluid and piecemeal. It would once become a mouth, then the palm of the hand, the weight of the thigh, then the lobe of an ear, the blankness of the eyes, the fold at the back, a firm grip on the swell of the back, a smooth shape you could cup in your hands, a funny taste you could poke with your tongue. His body disappeared into little toy objects spiralling outwards.

He was evidently enjoying himself too, grunting and kneading his palms into my chest and arms. I would come together to a sense of myself in the way that he was enjoying me. Suddenly I felt more in control. I felt that I had been the one in control all along, I was the one who had seduced him all the way to his bedroom, I was the one who was going to tick this off my list of encounters; I had authored this script, directed the show and played the part. How I had seduced a straight man, the scion of a business empire, no-names-please, I would tell with a twinkle in the eye.

I felt the urge to take control and reached my hand down and started stroking him. He was studiously avoiding my raging erection, making all the efforts not to look down there. I got myself over him and started my own expert dance. I pinned his hands down and started working myself into his neck, chest, digging my nose in his armpits, all the while constantly trying to push myself into him. I felt so certain of what I was doing, almost blind in the efficacy of my instinct. So this was what they must mean when they say you become more yourself than who you really are.

His surrender was instantaneous, almost too instantaneous and I felt his legs open out for me. A little taken aback at the sudden success of my moves, I dithered. His eyes were still closed but he grabbed my back and pushed me in closer, wrapping his legs around me. I could feel the warm, hungry pulsation from between his legs reaching out towards me. There could be no clearer signal than this and I immediately started to prepare myself. I knew from experience that it's in this awkward moment of putting on condom, grabbing your lube and the business delay necessary for the act, that all your efficiency and expertise counts. I saw that Jay had his eyes closed and was waiting in utter silence. His breathing was erratic and there were times when it seemed so shallow that he seemed not to be breathing at all. Like the devout at the moment of ushering in of the spirit, he was pure anticipation, totally still, as if any movement from him would dispel the image that had caught hold of in his mind. As soon as he felt me approach him, he pushed me into himself. I grabbed onto his shoulders, closed my eyes and began entering him with some care. I heard his voice quite a few pitches higher, almost like a girl's now, clearly pleading, 'Please don't fuck me!'

I hesitated. I couldn't understand. Did he want me to pull out? All my life I've picked up or been picked up from familiar places by guys who tell first, fuck later. Everybody knows their kink and every single act has been noted, measured and contracted from the decided anthropological categories of the sexual act. Everything has been rehearsed and *nothing* is ever left to chance or, god forbid, the heat of the moment. But right now I wasn't sure who I was with or what exactly he wanted from me. I looked for some other signs. Again he held me and pushed me, this time completely into himself. A controlled scream followed, 'Please don't fuck me!' I was all inside him now with hardly any effort from my own part. Yet he kept on making that ridiculous assertion. His eyes were closed but mine were wide open, looking at him slip into some role the exact meaning of which was known only to him. I couldn't take my eyes off the incredible drama happening right under me. Like an acolyte following movements that were mysterious to him I kept looking, following with the mechanical effort expected of me.

I wanted to stare hard enough to enter into his mind. I tried to feel the shape and contour of the role that I was being cast into. What did he want from me? Who was I to him in this moment? An elder cousin, a dirty old uncle, a boarding school head captain, who was it who had given this very straight guy the first taste of his twisted pleasures. Where had it happened? At some summer camp, at the back of the lawns in the school ground, here in this very room with someone from the family left to look after him? And at what point had persecution become pleasure . . .? My mind wandered in confusion.

He kept on moaning at the shocking realisation of his own submission. 'Oh you're fucking me!' followed by the pleading over and over not to, just not to fuck him. I have never been much interested in role-play but knew enough to know that this was not the straightforward script of masochism. What this guy needed was no, not a Dominator, because it didn't seem he wanted to be obedient or submissive. In fact, he was very fierce, even devious in getting what he wanted. His secret fantasy was like an attic he could run away to when he wanted to hide from the sunlight. No, what he needed was somebody who would take his fantasy and make it his own. Maybe one day he might just pick up a person who would be able to do that for him.

I kept on staring at him. For the second time during this eventful evening I found that I'd slipped into my favourite role in an otherwise awkward existence. The role of the audience. And I was witnessing for the second time this evening, the absurd tale of death and desire, this time at quarters which couldn't be more intimate. Inside the upstairs room of this family mansion where everything spoke of perpetuation and of carrying on, unfolded the sad-sweet tale of a poor-rich boy with the weight of clan, nay, race, loyalty on him, the younger son making way-out kinky sex in a house which still kept a floor for the dead one. And in this house, amidst all the objects that screamed of bad taste, was a painting of two girls loving each other that had somehow ended here for all the wrong reasons. A bit like this guy moaning under me – heir to the clan name, the sole survivor, the seed and sustenance caught in the blind grip of a secret, impossible pleasure.

It was time for me to close my eyes and retreat to myself. Since I did not have a place in his world or in its fantasies, it was time for me to surrender myself to my own senses. Surrender to the buzz in the ears, the rustle of the touch, the

colours that flashed as I closed my eyes and to the warmth
I could feel rising inside me. This was the only way, the
abstract one of sensation, through which I could have any
use for this guy here. And as I felt the warmth leaving his
body and slipping first down my legs and then covering me
all over, the life that he'd transmitted into me reached its
point of final surrender. I gave myself up to the final
breakdown of sound, sight, colour, feel and touch, and with
some final thrusts both of us collapsed into a grunting, cold
silence, each thankful for his separate desires.

~

In the morning, I woke in a state of panic, my mind running
the whole gamut of embarrassing confrontations that I would
have to go through on my way out of this crystal palace. I
got my clothes on and nudged Jay on the shoulder, who
woke up asking what time it was. I said it was six and that
I had work.

Sure, sure. Wrapped in a bedsheet, he got up to show me
the way out, but in his half-asleep state he seemed to be
struck by something. All of a sudden he turned around,
dived into his closet and returned with a tie.

He was handing it to me. A tie?!

'No, you're going for work. You should have one of
these.'

'No, no. I'm going to first go back to my place and then
to work. And I don't wear a tie to work.'

'Keep it.'

I stared at his puffed up, groggy face. Does the drama
never end for you?

I grabbed the tie and left. On my way out I did not bump into anyone except for the few servants who were getting about the day's work. I squeezed my way out of the driveway lined with swanky cars. It was one of those bleak summer mornings where early brightness carries over the dead weight of the day before and drops it over the head of today. The heat was unremitting.

~

Several months later I saw Jay again in a crowded pub. There was a rock gig happening on the first level and there he was on the third level terrace, beer in one hand, chatting up someone who looked like a failed model not yet aware of his failure. Later, when I was sitting at the bar I saw the model come up to him and say, 'Yeah we should definitely catch up.' They were soon walking out.

I remembered the tie that was meant to seal this pact of anonymity between us. It's still the most expensive tie I have.

Conference Sex

Ellen L.R.

How can I start this story? I have tried many times, unsuccessfully, to write it. The problem is that it all took place a long time ago. Since then, the sharp lines of immediacy have been replaced by fuzziness.

What is it, then, to look back on past intimacy? Sex has a memory which is quite different from the remembrance of other experiences – no more reliable, just different. Still, it's a fictionalised account, not *the truth* – I know this. And after all, even *the moment* lies because eroticism is all magnified senses . . . .

I should stop dithering uselessly and try one more time.

~

To cut a long story short, my story is about 'conference sex'.

Many have experienced it, I'm sure, and I did as well, when I travelled to attend a conference in South Asia. That conference itself can be verified, even now, years later, with an internet search. Some random details of conference presenters, keynote speakers, panels, and workshops are cached in the ways that are now familiar to web users. Of course, no record stands of what I call 'conference sex'. I need to look to my memory for that, but it is not similarly searchable.

One day of the conference must have passed before I met her: one day of very fine papers, speeches, posters, and discussions, all of which got through to me before we met, talked, and I became cocooned in a haze of feeling in which only she existed. That is, one day after my arrival at the conference, and two days before my departure, so it happened in a flash! I remember hoping that my face wouldn't give me away, that it wouldn't show how struck I was by her long black curly hair, expressive dark eyes, and crooked knowing smile. 'Hi,' she said briefly, when introduced. That smile. 'Hi,' I said back, nonchalantly. Her name was Shalini.

At the end of the day's sessions, I glanced around the room airily. No one in particular interested me, my eyes were saying; I'm just idly looking. 'Do you want to stretch your legs?' Shalini asked from behind me. Outfoxed, my face slipped its guard. I agreed eagerly.

We stepped out into a cold evening, two other conference participants with us. In fact, we were with people – lots of people, actually, as it is at a conference break at the end of the day when everyone is conferenced-out and dying to get away for a hot shower, hot dinner, cold beer – maybe secretly, even hot sex! When we all sat down together, I sat across from her so that I could observe her without being too conspicuous. Did she even like women? It was impossible to know. Presumed straight until declared otherwise, is the wisest way to go, of course. But I am getting ahead of myself.

~

Six or seven of us retreated with our ice-cold beer and munchables to a secluded spot where other conference attendees (i.e. those who were not welcome) would not spot us and ask to join us. Once settled, we puffed on our cigarettes and re-hashed the day's worth of good insight and argument and petty controversy. Not shy, she was in there with the rest of them, holding her own, laughing, teasing, rolling her eyes dramatically, always a little withholding so that you were still interested at what she must be keeping back. This kind of after-hours conference chat was familiar to me; it had its own conventions, nothing too daring. But, by degrees, I did become flustered. It was her manner. It was covertly flirtatious.

She looked at me for just that one second longer than could be accounted for, and she smiled with just that level of appeal that was more than nice. Small things, but some part of me knew and wondered whether to take it further, and if so, how. Very soon, a beery lot of the group got up and left us. There was a goodnatured sense of 'all good things' etc. amongst the rest, but I didn't want the evening to end. 'Where are you staying?' I asked her. Not far from my accommodation, it turned out. All very well, but what, conceivably, could be on offer? Not a nightcap, certainly. Maybe tea or coffee, but it was all horribly transparent. I felt gauche, choked by self-consciousness. Every possibility seemed to have the look of manipulation. Also acting against me was the setting. A conference was a place to display your smarts, to be self-aware, and droll and ironic – a place to forget about the body or to talk about it cerebrally, not to grub around with such carnal thoughts and invitations. Also, she was nobody's fool, clearly. She would have to consent to the invite on her own terms, unspoken as those terms were.

Delay resolved things. We said goodbyes all round, turning our cheeks perfunctorily to everyone until we came to each other. Something magical happened then. I bent to her, my breath frosting in the cold air. Her face reached up. Our arms moved us close into each other, and my face was in that wonderfully fragrant hair. Wiry to the touch, surprisingly dry, and dense, very dense. I could feel her face in my neck. A surge of excitement passed through me, uncontrollable, urgent. It was like nothing I had felt before. Quite simply, it was without my volition that I found myself pulling back blindly from her embrace and bending to her, mouth open. A kiss, madly, unthinkingly. Right there, in front of everyone who had not still left. Except, of course, sanity prevailed at the last minute. I found myself holding her by both arms, quite tightly, my face inches from her lips, my body quite tense with the effort to remember that it was not a good idea, that it was, in fact, a very bad idea to do this in public. It was too late, of course. One of the conference attendees was already adjusting her face into a smooth mask of unflappability meaning: I didn't see anything, I won't say anything. I hrrumphed, and Shalini – I can't remember what Shalini did. I only know that we made it up the dark, quiet road silently, back to our accommodation, pretending that we were all grownup, these things happen, not to worry, and it was good that it ended that way before it even began.

We reached and turned towards each other. 'A packed day tomorrow,' she sighed, 'I'm already exhausted. Will you attend everything?'

'Not everything,' I hedged.

'There's a market I've been meaning to visit. You're welcome to come if you're free,' she offered tonelessly, turning away at her door.

'Sure,' I said, 'I'll come around at ten or so.' Undoubtedly we had made a pact to be naughty, to play truant at the conference. In my mind, as serious conference attendees, this meant that we had broken the unspoken rule and were already intimate.

~

Nine thirty a.m. arrived, and I knocked on her door. She greeted me, recently bathed and perfumed, and more than a little overwhelming in a white tee and blue cotton shorts. Something did not seem right to me. She was clearly not ready for a trawl through the market. In fact, she didn't seem interested in it at all anymore. Instead, there was coffee, some cookies, and what looked like a deliciously long morning in ahead. I said nothing about the change of plans. The conference languished, abandoned.

Plenty of room on her bed for us to perch without touching. Somehow, though, the space between us kept closing imperceptibly, even as we sipped our coffee and chatted. She talked to me about her family – a sister who was doing well at work, was married, and parents who were still together and had the adorably South Asian parenting style of never letting go of their obligations towards their children. The words 'marriage' and 'husband' came and went in her conversation about her sister. We laughed together, and felt closer, but this was possibly still her conference persona. What was she like outside, in the everyday world? Kind, funny, well-meaning, impatient, sociable? Jolly, insecure, domineering, jealous, large-hearted? Grumpy, needy, driven, selfish, reclusive? No clue from our light-hearted patter.

It was my turn. I have always found the life story hard work and a bit of a sham, but this time, on her bed, in her cool scented room, it was more loaded. I rose sturdily to the challenge. Early ambitions (more sharply defined to make myself look purposeful); university degrees (passed over with a quick modesty); and my work (mentioned ruefully, because I wasn't unimaginatively and uncritically invested in it, was I?). She looked at me levelly throughout this performance, giving nothing away, only waiting for the next thing, perhaps something I had not said. We were toe to toe, almost adversarial.

Our coffee was done, the cups on the bedside table. We had slipped comfortably into lounging in silence, lying across the bed, our faces turned away from each other. Street noises filtered up vaguely. Feeling her move on the bed, I turned. She had turned and was looking right at me – just looking. We gazed at each other in silence for what seemed a minute, gradually unable to conceal our tension.

'Don't look at me like that,' she said jerkily. I continued to look at her. Desire, excitement – it was on my face, on her face, between us. 'Oh, great!' was all she said, heavily. Next, we had crawled into each other's arms. Her tongue in my mouth was gentle, her breathing quick. Eyes closed, I bit her lip, held her tongue in my mouth in a gentle, rhythmic suck. The room was very quiet except for our sighs, the hiss of our breathing. Her legs, moving restlessly, pulled my knee in between. A catch of breath, of pleasure, my leg squeezed between hers.

No time to think 'Is this really happening?' and 'Is this a good idea?' Our shirts were off, our trousers and shorts on the floor. On top of each other, nothing gentle about our kisses, my mouth inside hers, her lips stretched wide. That amazing hair was all over me when she pushed me roughly on to my back and kissed and bit my breasts. A snail trail of wet down to where I was waiting impatiently, and then her wonderful tongue, dividing me, flicking teasingly, and then settling instinctively into what I liked. I managed a quick gasped question about safe sex and being tested. But I was being pushed over the edge of the bed, my head angling back, my eyes unseeingly meeting the tacky picture on the wall. Pulling my legs up, her two fingers went in without asking – painful! Retreating, she pushed her fat thumb in. Gloriously fast, rough, and hard. My body shuddered under the impact.

The freshly showered scent of her was intoxicating. My tongue found her armpits, the back of her knees, the fragile shell of her ear. Our hands were interlaced. Her legs wrapped around my back, and I ground myself into her repeatedly, wildly. Reaching between us, I drove into her and we rocked against each other.

Surfacing many minutes later, we lay on the bed in a sweat, our breath coming fast. Conversation was out of the question. We had tested each other before with our probing life stories, then surprised each other with sex, and now what?

I strained against the awkwardness, the silence in the room. She was turned away, a slight unreadable smile on her face. It must have been hours since I entered that room – hours away from the conference, and for the first time I felt a guilty pang. 'No one saw you come in,' she said, her face still turned away, her voice coming from the end of a long tunnel. How she had anticipated my anxiety I will never know.

~

After a while she got up abruptly to check the time. A murmur – 'They'll start missing us in the next hour.' That was my cue to leave, I felt. All of this was utterly unfamiliar. I couldn't gauge her mood so I went with what I knew, which is that it's not wise to overstay one's welcome; people need their space; sex is sometimes just sex; and too much post-coital conversation is irritating.

I was pulling my clothes on, when she asked if I didn't want a shower. 'You can't go in smelling like that,' she smirked noncommittally. Completely inscrutable! I smiled and stumbled my way into the shower. A big league player, been around the block – it all sang in my head. Wanting more, was it reasonable or clingy? After just one morning of being together? Perhaps reasonable, but maybe wait on her to make that move?

Her shower smelled like her. I pretended to ignore these small pricks of familiarity and the creeping yearning they produced. The glass shower cubicle beaded over as I turned the hot water on, then faded from view as my eyes squinted shut against the shampoo suds. Red and steaming, I felt blindly for the soap and then, not finding it, opened one eye. I started back! She was standing silently, ghostly, right there, just outside the shower cubicle. Not saying anything, just looking. 'Hi,' I shouted above the din of the water, 'Want to come in?'

Without answering, she dropped her towel, stepped on it, and slid into the shower. Beautiful, those eyes still more than a match for me. Her composed quiet was unnerving. Instinctively, I crossed my arms over my breasts. Her sodden hair curled over her shoulders. She took the soap from me proprietarily, turned me against the wall, and soaped my back. Hands flattened against the wall, I let myself feel the gentle wash of her hand on my body, the hot water running off and pooling at my feet. A sharp push at both knees, and my legs were spread expertly from behind. I turned, not wanting to be this helpless with someone I barely knew, but her hands were on my bottom, soaping in between and then running, practised, between my legs. Two slippery fingers slid into me, not painful like before, and quite determined to do what they had not been allowed to, before. Once again, I was surprised by the force of her hands which had been small and inconspicuous in the conference halls. Her left arm snaked around me, her hand pinching my breasts hard, making its way down my soapy body to between my legs where it rubbed insistently while her right hand moved in and out of me.

I felt the pleasure of it, and also the fact that it would stay there, not peak. She was too uncanny, or maybe it was the idea of being so intimate with someone I hardly knew, at a conference where I was to be respectable and be respected, not on my back. The bed was one thing, but the shower? I didn't overthink it – at least I don't think so. 'Shalini' I gurgled, turning, before she kissed my lips shut hard, the water running into our mouths. I held both her hands firmly away from me, then brought her in close to me, letting her feel the tenderness I had hidden. She didn't protest, but I could feel her body tense with resentment and contained excitement. After a while she relaxed against me, then moved away and rinsed herself briskly. A growing sense of hurt and disappointment between us which neither would acknowledge.

We dressed silently. I kissed her cheek, saying I would see her at the conference. She saw me to the door unsmilingly. I almost ran to my room, picked up the pens, plastic folders, coloured agendas, pamphlets and books I may not read after the conference. My heart was pounding. What just happened? Once at the venue, I slipped into the room, unnoticed I hope. A couple of heads turned towards me, but I made a great show of pouring myself some coffee. Was my hair wet? Did I smell like her? Was her hair on my clothes? For the next hour I sat tightly on my chair, these thoughts churning in my head. A while later, I relaxed and allowed myself to remember how delicious it had been.

~

I had not quite missed everything, but a good chunk of the day had passed me by. I joined in with false hilarity, nods and murmurs while the others discussed what had gone before. It was a busy conference, I might not have been missed. It was only after lunch that I dared to look around for her. Not at the table with the big names; not at the table with random people; and not at the table with friends who had planned to meet at the conference. Where was she?

The post-lunch panels had me nervy and looking around. I went in and out of each, trying not to appear as though I was looking for someone. By tea, I had still not found her. No phone number to ring, only a door to knock on.

Too agitated to concentrate, I went in search of her. There was her door, remote, not answering, like her. Had I upset her? Was there something she had expected of me that I didn't give? It was a conference, I reassured myself; no one expects anything like this, and there are no rules for behaviour.

~

I left the country a day or two later, still not having heard from her. The sore spot in my heart healed soon enough. Years later, quite randomly, a friend had been introduced to her. In the first five minutes, they had found me on the map of people they knew, like all South Asians do. She had asked after me politely and given her best. But not her email address.

I Hate Wet Tissues

Satya

Darkness did it.
Or did it?

He and I are walking the scorching streets, looking for a place to have chilled beer. This town sleeps in the afternoon but we are looking for even a tiny shack. Feeling like brothers, out in the world, knowing where we are going. Not a word between us. Pounding the streets. Feeling one.

He is big. Broad shouldered. Large hands. Inside his cargo pants. Shuffling his pack of wet tissues. He'd make a beautiful Transman when he gets on T and removes those breasts. Having removed mine twelve years ago, and nurtured a thick beard over fifteen, qualified me.

I know him the minute I see him. We hug. His arms enclose my torso fully, but he keeps his chest to himself. The palm of my hand knows the binder he is wearing under those layers of clothing and we let the moment pass quickly. He says this is impossible to do in Lahore what you have done in Delhi. How did you?

How did I?

~

The 8x6 room is not enough. He puts his olive green bag down in the corner. It's going to be beer.

~

He and I are walking the scorching streets, looking for a place to have chilled beer. His black polished military boots make a deeply satisfying bodily sound; my Bata chappals feel so limp.

In the dark, seven-table shed, men are drinking. The shed is silent with the sounds of drinking. Sounds of small glasses on old wooden tables. Sounds of meat bones falling on aluminium plates. Lungis over knees, legs apart under tables, deep dark brown skin, moulding shoulder bones and chest muscles, glistening hard in the heat. The smell of sweat, nestled in body hair. And then mixed in, the smell of meat. The alcohol wetting the lips. And moustaches. Of men and transmen. Alike.

~

There is enough between us now. The 8x6 enclosure can prevent only that much from happening. We sit side by side on the 6x2 bed. And into the afternoon I tell him how I did it. He looks upon me as if looking upon his father. How many sons we give birth to in the anonymity of 8x6 rooms ... But he wants to witness with his own eyes. The chest hair sprouting from the scars of my mastectomy. The meatiness of the constructed penis. The bloodiness and spread of the glans. But unzipping my trousers is not as easy as unbuttoning my shirt. There is another coming out that I know will seal this connect forever. I am brave again. I tell him that my father is from Karor Laalison in Pakistan. And that my mother's father is from Lahore. And her mother from Jalarpur Jatta. I look into his eyes. He should have worn some kajal in them. He runs his fingers playfully through my hair and says we should do Karor Laalison together someday.

~

Will you stay?
He snuffles into a wet tissue.

~

Rules of engagement: I am not allowed to open his shirt or take his pants down. Yes, I can kiss him. On his face but not his lips. Between desire and the risk to his self, we agree that I can rub him on his packer without touching him directly. The rest can flow. And we can call stop when we want to.

Spooning is a good place to start. He presses his ass onto my crotch and the movement rises through my spine and lands my lips on the back of his neck. The wetness turns him around and he breathes into my chest. Where should I hold him? I remember what it was for me. When you are not your nude body. When your nude body is not your desire. And when the impossibility of this desire, to inhabit and act through this body, can lead you to a bottle of sleeping pills.

Who is more qualified to protect him than I? Against my own desire to suckle his breasts, as breasts ... enter his vagina, as vagina ... to tear open his shirt and the layers of clothing under ... to turn him around and onto his knees ... to enter his mouth against the thrusts of my own grasp of his face ... to pin him, take him and go, go, go ...

If the shame of these thoughts was not visible to him, it was only because I lay naked, exhausted, nestled near the bound chest of a fully-clothed man. He made a very satisfying lover and it's true that the hold of large hands can be very substantial. Was that a look of love? The look of being somewhere else . . . was he seeing with his naked eyes the possibility of becoming a man . . . could there have been a more honest way to tell him how *this* man had become a man . . .

He dresses my feet with his boots and comes up my naked body in swirling strokes of his tongue . . . how strange; these boots make me stand on my legs again, and fill me with a desire that I have never known in Bata chappals . . . but the turn to ride is his now and he wants to show me something new. It happens again and again, rhythms multiply, play begins and ends and brotherhood deepens.

~

He says he can't take my sweat anymore.
Cold water on all this love is not our idea of an ending.
I ask him to wipe me with his pack of wet tissues.

~

He says this is impossible to do in Lahore what you have done in Delhi.
How did you?
How did I?

~

Department of Plastic and Reconstructive Surgery
Government Teaching Hospital
Delhi; sorry, New Delhi.

The trolley bed is wheeled through the corridors. My body is naked under a long single garment touching my ankles, with buttons in the centre and running through the length of it. I have been on T for over two years now and am taken for a man. Even when lying on this trolley bed. Even with this single thin green garment, worn by hundreds before me, lying crumpled over my body, communicating against my deepest discomfort its contours to the attendant pushing the trolley and nearest to me.

'Kya hua tha?'

'Matlab?'

'Matlab, bachpan mein kissine . . .?'

'. . . kheench diye the?'

'Hain . . .'

'Par aadmi ke mamme itne bade kabhi dekhe nahi.'*

His crotch brushes against the trolley frame, pushing it further towards the OT. As the largeness between his legs comes near my face, recedes and moves closer again, I meet his gaze; we know we are family and I am not alone anymore. The dread of what they call Sex Reassignment Surgery lessens in the assurance of his presence. His hand comes closer to my head as he wheels the bed and I turn my cheek to rest it on his thin hairy fingers.

---

* 'What happened?'
  'Meaning?'
  'I mean, when you were a child, did someone . . .?'
  '. . . yank on them?'
  'What . . .?'
  'But I've never seen such big tits on a man before.'

As he leaves me in the pre-op room, I ask, *'Kahan karte ho?'*

*'Pehle yeh karvalo, phir tumhe wahan le jaaunga.'**

~

Under the diagnosis section of my papers, it reads: 'Gynecomastia' – a condition defined by medicine as, 'The abnormal development of large mammary glands in males, resulting in breast enlargement'. The diagnosis gives Dr K a place to hide, and without his knowing, it communicates my truth: indeed, I am a man with large breasts. Dr K has done some rather fine line drawings around them, to mark out the sites of incision. When the knife will touch skin along these black markings and remove the subcutaneous fat under it, I will be turned into a man some more. With the black marker in one hand, and a wet tissue in the other, Dr K draws and erases, and redraws and erases repeatedly around my breasts, till he has the lines he wants. The friction of the erasure and the rough wetness of the wet tissue makes my nipples erect. Not all erections are desired. And some, like these, even detested. Especially by the one to whom the breasts belong. To whom the nipples belong. To whom this body belongs. But Dr K is as stoic as ever. Not a twitch, nor a freezing of his drawing movement, nor a blink of an eye. His crotch remains as flat and unremarkable as it was when he entered.

The blackened wet tissue is thrown on the floor and my eyes are blindfolded. I am made to stand against a blank

---

* 'Where do you do it?'
  'First get this over with, then I'll take you there.'

wall. Of my naked, sagging, large breasts, with lines imprinted on the skin from the self-fabricated elastic binder I have worn for years, a photograph is clicked. Without a flash. And then some others.

~

How is it that doctors can do this? Is it because they touch so many breasts, finger so many cunts and lift so many dicks everyday? Didn't my breasts get in the way of his mathematical calculations about how much tissue would be removed from where? When they touch their lover's lips and cup their genitals, do they see the bodies they have handled all day long? Other breasts, other cunts, other dicks? How does so much body every day, and sex, mix? But this seemed like fun. I could make a game of it and draw red lines around my lover's breasts one day. And when my career as an artist begins to dry up, I could make some performance art out of it: get on stage; have my lover draw thick purple lines around my big, drooping, imprinted upon, prosthetic breasts, with their erect nipples in the middle of large dark areolas; and then ask her to photograph me.

With a flash. For performance.

~

The morgue isn't anything I know of from Hindi films. Or even Hollywood.

But sex in the morgue of a Delhi Government Teaching Hospital can compete with European Art House porn.

Rules of engagement: He is not allowed to open my shirt or take my pants down. Yes. He can kiss me. On my face but not my lips. Between desire and the risk to my self, we agree that I will suck him. The rest can flow. And we can call stop when we want to. And one more thing: he wants to face the bodies in the morgue as I blow him.

I don't believe this already; He takes my hand and guides it through the open zip of his attendant's shorts. He is 5 feet 9 inches and for my 5 feet 3, I have to go down on him. Extracting a semi-erect dick lying on one side is a special pleasure; far better than lifting a flaccid one that lies in the centre or is rested upward and below the navel. I am extracting his, from within very tight underwear, under a very tight pair of shorts, through a very short length of zip. It's circumcised. And thick. And long enough for quick, short strokes. He aims it against the inside of my right cheek and the saliva drips as he emerges and goes in again. His arms are lifted and held together behind his neck. He is a man with that self-assuredness that his organ needs no support. And that it can have a life of its own. And so the strength of his thrusts is very particular, very pointed, very powerful. His dirty white shirt is open to the last button and his dirty white shorts are just below his crotch, half-covering his very tight buttocks. And the dirty whiteness has a strange glow about it. Suddenly the smell of dead embalmed bodies hits me, over and above the smell of my saliva on his organ, and over and above the smell of his piss in his underwear. The movement in my stomach begins to rise and I can taste the dal and palak paneer and my night medicines in my mouth. Vomit from fellatio in a morgue, vomit dripping from the phallus, vomit held in the bottom of the very tight underwear of an almost naked, standing man.

But so many dead dicks, of men lying behind me, that don't witness my vomit.

I can't take the sight of my half-digested food and pills on his stuff. I wish I had a wet tissue. But this, and my increasing sense of fainting, turn him on further and he puts all of it back in my mouth again. As if in there forever. With his emaciated body, naked to the bone. I have less and less strength in my legs and my heart is sinking; I want to close my eyes and he takes complete control. Holding me up from my armpits, taking my full weight at his wrists and shoulders, half bent over me, he moves like madness, in and out of me. That I am fully on the ground and hardly moving is not going to stop him. His movements are a hysteria now. I hear him say *'Abbe! Behosh mat ho! Murde ke mooh mein paani chudwaega kya?! Utthja!'**

---

* 'Hey! Don't faint! You think I want to come in a dead man's mouth?! Get up!'

Screwing with Excess

Vinaya Nayak

'What is essential is invisible to the eye,' said Antoine de Saint-Exupery, and he could have been talking about V. V wasn't essentially beautiful. He was short, stocky and adored and embraced his natural smells. But what he had was a bewitching after-sex smile; it was still seductive, luxurious and fat. He was quite unbearable otherwise, and you had to fuck him a lot to get him to look fuckable again. For my best friend L, it was that very incompleteness that made him attractive. This wasn't strange because L collected the weary, the unusual and the extraordinary among the masses.

At the time, L and I were on an adventure. We had a little room to live in, a small income to spend unwisely and a pack of cards. We did everything together; we tried on dresses, blouses and saris, wore mundus and made sarongs with lungis. On Sundays, we bought second-hand books on the streets, dressed in seedy clothes with kohl in our eyes and then read to each other all night long. And then nearly at dawn we cuddled. That's right, we were not having sex; you see, I was straight and he was gay. Well, not strictly, just at the edges of those boundaries, always threatening to spill over, but balancing rather breathtakingly.

~

One evening, we snuck into a film society's screening; the film had been the usual subtitled fare of post-war angst and soul search, much, much sex and many flashbacks to peaceful days. It was disturbing and disturbingly titillating. I cried at the end of the film, you understand, for all the sadness in the film. L cried too, he did that, he cried about films, not about life, mind you. Our display of cinematic stimulation must have been emphatic; the patroness of the film society, let's call her M, was moved enough to invite us to her house to discuss the film.

M, the daughter of a very famous actress from the 40's and the 50's, had a very expensive and largely garish house. She sat us down beneath a huge poster of her mother's film and left to get into "something a little less ... " her silver-bangled hands tinkling jaggedly in the aftermath of that expansive gesture of her hands. The poster, not of one of M's mother's more well-known films, was most of the wall; the actress had carried a character from her teens to an aging grandmother, and on the poster she looked pruned and shrivelled like she had never been in life. There were, of course, other photos of her, the black-and-white ones where she was young and stunning, framed and placed on small end tables along with much knick-knack.

M came back wearing a pink silk singlet and pyjamas that

revealed all those fat little tyres that the Shambalpuri tussar had lovingly embraced. She walked towards us unfurling a long black shawl that I can only assume was cashmere. She wrapped it around herself and sat down next to L, neatly, like a large geisha. She ran her fingers through L's at the time luxurious hair and said, 'So? Wine?' We said yes, I made the small well-brought-up noise volunteering to fetch, she shook her head ever so slightly and whispered. A girl, her 'domestic,' appeared magically, carrying a tray with four glasses of white wine and a plate with small cubes of cheese. L accepted his wine and gushed about the slender wine glasses and the Auroville-esque earthy-looking platter of cheese. I popped a piece of what turned out to be Amul cheese in my mouth and stared at the fourth glass. 'Who is the fourth glass for, M?' asked L, deftly avoiding a cube of cheese. 'Ah, my son, V, I hope he will join us soon, he would love to meet you,' she said pointedly to me. I smiled a cheesy smile, L looked aghast and rolled his eyes at me. 'He is a little shy, but I want him to meet sensitive young people like you two.' M discreetly wiped her mouth; I self-consciously dragged out a disgusting piece of tissue from my jeans and dabbed at my lips. Meanwhile, M had oriented herself towards L and was smiling, he had started a long monologue about wines, 'Napa valley . . . now even *Nashik* . . . but French wines . . .' and he took a graceful swallow, exposing to M's adoring eyes his beautiful long neck. I don't know how L could be so confident talking about wines, all we had glugged was Golconda and the odd cheap Goan port.

L had moved himself to the floor; he had this way of caressing his collarbones that made him look so desultorily sexy, he was doing that now. He wasn't actually sitting on the floor, he seemed to be hovering just above it, like some great gazelle moving in slow motion. M was in the throes of excitement already, she had let the shawl slip to reveal a bit of her shoulders and an arm that had just a hint of fat over robust muscle and sinew.

Sitting next to her, I looked like a teenage frump. I wasn't unattractive, I was actually classically beautiful; small and thin from my current malnutrition but I had long hair that was lusciously raging against the destruction I was subjecting my body to. All the smoking had caused the baby fat from my face to vanish, I had high cheekbones, and large kohl-lined eyes, ergo classically beautiful. Except when I smiled. I had an obviously fake smile and often, to L's amazement, it even touched my eyes. I did not know how to smile; it had always been toothy and extra wide. I had the deepest dimples amongst my less-dimpled siblings and cousins and this fake smile was developed from winning contests with them. When I was uncomfortable, like now, I pushed my cheeks up so much that my dimples were craters. I felt like that gorgeous French girl in *Bitter Moon*, who gets uglier and uglier when her lover subjects her to petty humiliation.

I had reasons to be in that filmic moment right now. M was almost whispering into L's ears, I could no longer hear her, while L, for no logical or physiological reason, was studiously engaged in this game of seduction. I sat there with a stupid grin, and hoped that V would appear soon and was not a figment of this aging diva's imagination. M was beautiful and so was her-mother-the-actress, chances were the son was beautiful as well. I firmly believed in genetics.

~

Our wine glasses were empty and every cube of ghastly cheese on the platter had been eaten by me, the one nice cold glass of wine was perspiring invitingly, M had not offered to refill, and I was all cheesy-mouthed and thirsty; as yet no sighting of V. L was being revolting with M, he was fingering her shawl saying, 'You know M, as a child I always thought cashmere had something to do with Kashmir!' She laughed a short pretty laugh, 'You say the most naive things, we shouldn't let people think you don't know about all this.' He curled up to her like a cat. He was such a glutton for beautiful things.

I got up from my chair to explore that large room. I picked up one of those frames with the actress's photograph. 'M, your mother was such a great beauty, almost ethereal.' Ethereal, I had read, was a favourite description for the actress. 'Yes,' she said, just a little brusquely. 'Where is that son of mine?' For the first time that day she raised her voice and called out to V. Then when she heard no reply she left the room, to fetch him, I assumed.

'What the fuck are you doing?' I pinched L. 'Are you going to fuck her? That's your type, the aging diva? So I can expect sex when I am about seventy?'

'Shut up, she is so lonely and beautiful.'

'And cheap! That was Amul cheese for god's sake!'

'Yet you are the only idiot who ate it.'

'Yeah, what do you want me do when you are fawning on her like some gigolo, I was bored. If you touch that shawl one more time ever so gently you think she is going to wrap it around your shoulders . . .'

'Then you flirt with her, why are you sitting there like an egg? Have you felt that shawl, it is beyond exquisite.'

'So this is a shawlgasm!' L had a thing for shawls so bad that he hated summers. 'Doesn't she know you are gay?'

'I have told you this before; it doesn't matter, especially to a woman of a certain age and type. You only seem to get it at some academic level.'

'So let's have a studious fuck L, I will cram like hell for it,' I hissed.

'I can't talk to you when you are like this. We can sleep together, only it can't mean what you want it to mean.'

~

M walked back into the room as though on cue saying, 'This is my son, V . . .' I couldn't see him at first, he was standing behind his tall mother, then he emerged. M had clearly not mated with her genetic match. I heard L take in a short sharp breath of desire, V was the best of the misfits that we had met in recent times. M introduced us, V shook the tip of my fingers, and raised his hand to L in a short wave. L's hand almost instinctively went to his collarbones, 'Hi!' So impish, so appealing.

M let L stand in front of V for about twenty seconds, then like a seasoned pro, 'Come,' she said unfurling her great black shawl and flinging it casually on the sofa, 'let me show you my sari collections, I even have a few that Ma wore.' To her son she said, 'I hope you will take care of the young lady?' L was torn, but he made his choice: 'Do you collect shawls as well?' as they left the room.

V looked me over from head to toe, did not linger over my breasts, then he picked up the wine glass and flopped on the chair, 'Are you two together?'

Obviously not, he is going into your mother's bedroom! I thought, but said, 'No, just friends.'

He smiled, 'he is a homo you know?'

So astute, 'I know.'

'My mother is so foolish,' he jeered, and drowned the wine in a single gulp. 'Come, I am not allowed to smoke in the living room.'

We walked out to the balcony at the end of the hall; it was a beautiful night and the house sat on Banjara hills and had the most fantastic view of the city. 'Stars above, stars below and stars in the house,' I said.

'Are you flirting with me?'

I wasn't, I was mortally afraid of flirting, the only flirting I ever did was with gay men, where there was no fear being taken seriously. 'What if I am?' I dimpled.

'You want to smoke?' He smiled smugly and with a flourish took out a pack of Charminar and a kitten matchbox from his pockets.

'Yes, please.' He put two cigarettes between his lips.

He struck a match, he struck two and two again. 'Allow me,' I said, touching his shoulder gently, just like M had L's. He handed me one of the cigarettes and dropped the matchbox in my hand. I put the cigarette between my lips and lit it, with a single strike of the match. Then I took the other one hanging from his mouth and lit it with my cigarette and handed it to him. I was only missing a hat to doff at him.

'Tanks,' he said, not 'thanks'; 'tanks' like I had just handed him his ball at recess. This was going to be tough.

'So what do you do?' I asked.

'I am going to be a hero. Opposite Ramya; we will start shooting next month. I am building my body now.'

Wow! He is going to be a hero?

'Wow, you are going to be a hero!'

'Yes, I will start in Telugu, and then who knows, one day Bollywood,' he made a flying plane gesture with his hand.

That flying hand came to rest on my shoulder. 'So you want to fuck a hero?'

Not so tough after all, I thought, and smiled at him, the moon would be lost in my craters.

~

'Come,' he said sounding just like mama M, holding out his right hand while chucking his still-lit cigarette on the floor with his left. I stubbed out my cigarette self-consciously on the floor and took his hand. I let him lead me into his surprisingly sparse bedroom. One large bed, a beautiful old chest of drawers, one Bombay fornicator near a large window and a large mahogany dressing table with a beautiful mirror lit from three sides. He seemed to sense my bewilderment. 'This was my grandmother's room, I shifted here when I decided to become a hero.'

He stood behind me, his hammy hands cupping my breasts, 'So do you want to do it on D Devi's bed?' suddenly making the deal very, very sweet. I turned around and put my arms around his neck, arched my back slightly and raised my lips to his.

'Not like this,' he said, yanking my hands from his neck. 'We have to do it like a film, you are the vamp and I am the hero, seduce me,' he said, jumping on that bed. 'Come on.' He arranged himself on the bed, his hands behind his head, the bulge in his pants almost bigger than his head.

This was getting to be too much work. I wondered what L was doing to earn his cashmere shawl.

'Ok, give me a song.'

'*Yeh mera dil, pyaar ka deewana*' he shouted back urgently. I moved to a little stool in front of the mirror and sat down, turned on the lights and looked at my reflection. I was not me, I couldn't be, I was D Devi – well not really, I was just about to fuck her grandson – it is not that kind of a story. I was Devisque – still too weird. L had the other day performed a whole medley of vampish songs for me, so I was L – yes, L could very well do this.

Still on the stool, I turned towards the hero and slowly parted my long, long legs (L's phantom legs) then very demurely brought my legs together. I pulled out the pencil that was keeping my hair in a loose knot. My hair, always ready to play a role, fell heavily over my shoulders, I heard him take in a breath.

I stood up, hummed the opening line, the only line I knew, *yeh mera dil, pyaar ka deewana.*

'Okay now strip, slowly.' Bulgy boy

'You first, the vamp has you naked and angry in her house of disrepute,' I said.

'Her what?'

'Brothel ... whore house ... *kotha*'

'Okay!' It took him about thirty seconds to strip. He had a nice body, nearly six packs, maybe just a pair short. He had very distasteful hero-like biceps but otherwise a rather lean body. His legs were also very leanly muscled, his thighs in particular, taut and with deep sinewy cuts. His penis was a nice size for a man of that stature. 'Okay, now me!' I reached to remove my sweatshirt. 'Slowly, slowly,' he said urgently.

I removed my sweatshirt; beneath it I was wearing a blue buttoned-down peasant blouse, and a pair of jeans. I decided to remove my blouse first. The top button, then three more. I paused, slipped my right hand inside my shirt and caressed my left breast; he made an urgent movement tightening his thighs, tauter lines. I was quite excited myself. I undid the rest of the buttons and turned my back to him and let the shirt fall away from my body.

'Turn around.'

'Not yet.' I heaved my breasts and arched my back. I have very expressive shoulder blades a mere flick and they would sing; a narrowish waist, and on it I always wore a thin silver chain. I heard him get off the bed and come toward me, he hugged me hurriedly, rubbing his penis against my thighs and my butt.

The hero was seduced, the vamp had won.

He unhooked my bra, quite expertly, and gruffly pushed aside my hair and bit my neck, a long hard vampire-like suck. I made a little noise of pain and pleasure. He covered my naked breast with his hammy, clammy hands. 'Follow the plan, remove your clothes facing me.' He gruffly turned me toward him and kissed me, kiss actually a misnomer; he enveloped every bit of my lips, teeth and tongue inside his fat lips. Wet, painful and my cunt informed me that it liked this very much.

He went back to his bed, I removed my bra, my jeans and my underpants; I was slow but absolutely without hesitation. Divested of my clothes, I stood before him.

'You are actually hot; my mother usually brings me such ugly girls.'

Brings him! So this was hooking.

'Yes, I am, we better get on with this, friend,' I pointed to his bulge, 'you don't seem to have much time.' I climbed into bed with him. I was a little tired of the role play. Hero-vamp, whore-customer even that little bit of master-slave. I got into bed with him and turned on my side, then aggressively cupped his balls while thrusting my tongue into his left ear. He was moaning and his butt was quivering. I got on top of him. 'Condoms?' I demanded.

'Really?'

'Yes, really! It is my *dhande ka vasool.*'*

'I don't have any, so we have to do it like this only.' Gleefully.

---

*'Yes, really! It's the rules of my trade.'

'Wait here, I have some,' I said confidently. I knew that L always had a pack in his cavernous bag. I pulled on my sweatshirt and went out to fetch them. I found L sitting outside, smoking and reading. He also carried books in that bag. He was reading a slim volume of what looked like poetry.

'What? Done already?' we said to each other in sync.

'Yes ya, we had the most straightforward missionary sex and then she had some giant orgasm or faked it, took a pill and asked me to wait outside for my little friend. You?'

'Mama does not allow smoking in the living room you know!'

'Hmmm, are you done?' taking a long drag.

'Ongoing, your M is something else, apparently they do this a lot, you know, she gets girls for him. Why does it feel so sordid?'

'They are rich, we are poor, and you are actually a good little girl,' he hugged me affectionately.

'Right!' I huffed, 'give me a condom!'

'Here,' diving into his bag to drag a pack out. 'He is hot though, no? So short, muscular and those fat lips . . .'

'He looks and smells like a pig!'

'Why are you going through with it then?'

'I am a feminist! I can't be a tease, ya! He was sort of interesting when he got all masterful!'

'How hot! Did you see that smile though, so sexy!'

'That bit is true!'

'He is so my type.'

'I know.'

'I know you know, my little feminist! So, you need some help in there?'

'No! But yes please,' I smiled my first genuine smile of the day.

~

V was lying exactly as I had left him, his penis seemed to be moving back and forth like a periscope skimming above the water. 'I thought you had run away!'

'I brought back a little surprise. You remember L from earlier today, he wants to join us. What say he can be the villain, I will be the vamp and you are of course, the hero?'

'Okay, but only you can do things to me not the homo.'

While I was making righteous noises, L said, 'That sounds fine. I will not even be the villain, I will be the *kaneez*, the vamp's *sakhi*. What say we tie you up, you are here unwillingly, hero!'

'Okay.'

I looked for something to tie him up with. I found a gorgeous silk kimono inside one of the drawers of the dresser.

'My grandmother's,' V said quickly.

I nodded and took out the thick yellow silk sash and while L winced, I suppose at my treating this beauteous thing so indelicately, I secured our hero's hands, tying them together and then to an arch on the top of the headboard. L stood behind the headboard and started taking off his clothes. I climbed on top of the bed and straddled V. I arched my back and stretched by hands behind me for the condoms that I had left at the foot of the bed. Both L and V had a good view of my cunt. My stomach in that yogic pose was very taut and my breasts were standing up and pointing north. They were not large, but the large dark aureoles made them look bigger. The surprising contrast of their darkness and the whiteness of my breast could be very beautiful. I felt young and ripe. I reached for the pack of condoms and straightened up swiftly. I pulled out one and tore open the condom wrapper with my teeth. Then I bent down, letting my long curly hair linger over his torso, gave his penis one short suck and then sheathed it.

'Some more sucks, please, please,' he begged.

'Later!' I said.

I looked at L standing behind the headboard. He had stripped down. He was a beautiful angular creature, all long legs and limbs. Sharp jaws, sharp collarbones, and sharp eyes below arched eyebrows. Right now, those eyes were looking at me hungrily. I had never seen that before. Hero boy was groaning, I kissed his chest and bit his nipples, he moaned more. The lips of my cunt were caressing his madly gesticulating penis, which was urgently trying to find me. I decided to help him out; with my right hand I guided him inside me. His whole body shuddered; I made small circling motions from my hips. A whoosh sound when my cunt pulled away a little from his penis.

We went on like this for just a few seconds, then he urgently raised his buttocks and made a final thrust, I tried to hurry to the climax but he got there before me, he came in a giant shudder and I felt him go flaccid immediately. He was done, and so well done that he smiled that hot little smile and went right to sleep. Hands still tied to the bed post.

I shrugged at L. 'That's that I guess,' and got off him.

~

L came out from behind the headboard. And sat on the bed and started stroking V's thighs. V was coming alive, at least his penis was. L removed the condom and tossed it to the floor. He bent down on V and began to suck his penis. Long deep sucks, I could swear that V's penis was near his throat and every time V moaned, L withdrew, and V moaned more. L came up for air and whispered to me, 'Kiss him or something.'

I got to the head of the bed and started kissing the comatose boy; I licked his face, those fat lips, yanked his hair and pulled his head back, he screamed in pain, I bit his neck hard and sucked at it. Meanwhile L was playing hide and seek with V's penis. He would suck him till he was very near coming and then withdraw. I did not leave V much time to complain; when L withdrew I kissed V. He was not really awake. V turned to me, suddenly perfectly lucid and begged me, 'Please stop for a second, let him finish the blow then you can go down on me.'

Not so homophobic now, I see. I let them get on and sulked on the Bombay fornicator, V had pulled himself up and was sitting on the bed, and L was being ridiculously limber. He had climbed down on V so much that L's ass was at V's face. V was hungrily licking it, while L was finishing up with the blow. One more giant shudder and lucky V came again. And like his switch-off button had been activated, nodded back to sleep.

'The boy's on drugs,' L smiled at me, getting off the bed.

'Let's get out of here,' I said to him.

'Not yet,' he whispered and stood me up. 'You were so beautiful, my dear,' and he kissed me gently. Our mouths did not part, it was a peck; I moved my head back. He leaned into me, kissed me, licking the corners of my mouth, dragging his tongue slowly over my lips. He was pushing his tongue into my mouth, like tasting a fresh, moist brownie.

'Don't start what you won't finish.'

'I am a feminist, I can't be a tease ya,' he smiled.

He draped his arms around my naked waist, tucking his thumbs into the silver chain at my back, and we danced as he moved me around the room. 'We are dancing naked in D Devi's room, and you are more beautiful, B. Those eyes speak all the time. They know what you are going to feel even before you feel them.'

'Filmy ya,' I was resting my head on his shoulders.

'Inspired.'

'I love you my little B,' he said.

'I know.'

'I am so turned on by you right now; I want to lick you all over.'

'I am feeling particularly dry right now.'

He licked my neck, gave me small butterfly kisses across the breast, turned me around and caressed my back, he danced me to the Bombay fornicator and sat me down.

'Fornicating on a fornicator,' I said. 'Do you think D Devi imagined we would realize the actual use for her chair?'

'Darling, why do you think she had this in her room?'

'Everybody is always in an orgy in your head!'

'Everybody *is* in an orgy in their heads.'

He placed my legs on top of the freakish long hands of the fornicator. Then he went down on me. Licking my clitoris in quick sharp licks, he put his tongue inside me, moving it around like a fastidious wine taster – I had a fever, I was burning up – and then as the pace quickened, smaller, faster licks and I finally climaxed. It was like smoking the first cigarette of the day.

'Penis is never this good,' I gasped.

'Darling, I have always told you your cunt likes tongue.'

'What about you?' I asked weakly.

'What good manners,' he smiled kindly, 'I am the *kaneez* remember, and the *kaneez* only gives.'

~

V let out a loud moan, started chanting his grandmother's name. L and I grinned. We untied him, he woke up a bit; L shushed him back to sleep and covered him up. He even gave him a nice long kiss, 'Sleep well, Quasimodo.'

I looked at L, he turned to meet my gaze, 'Stop staring, two a day is all I can eat.'

'Disgu, let's go home,' I said, getting dressed. He followed suit.

'I am going to burn that sweatshirt,' he threatened.

'Then give me back my shawl!' We slipped out and made our way to the door, 'Wait, I forgot something, wait for me outside,' I said to him. I went back to the living room and took the black cashmere shawl that M had left draped on the sofa.

L was standing outside and smoking, I draped the shawl on him. 'Here, payment.'

'I knew you went back for this.'

'Of course you knew!'

Contributors

Abeer Hoque is a Nigerian-born Bangladeshi-American writer and photographer. She doesn't want none but kisses. 'Jewel and the Boy' is an excerpt from her novel in progress, *Memory Alone*. See more at olivewitch.com

Anirban Ghosh studied animation film design at the National Institute of Design, Ahmedabad after graduating in Mass Communications from St. Xavier's College, Kolkata. Storytelling fascinates Anirban as he uses illustration reportage, sequential art, short films and documentaries to narrate tales on gender, sexuality, human rights as well as other mundane tales of growing up and the world around.

Annie Dykstra has been living in Delhi for four years and, in that time, has been lucky enough to over-indulge her fetish for swimming pools. It has also helped her explore the endless erotic possibilities of sofas (especially ones created in the 1970's) and a fetish for the love poetry of seventh-century Tamil poets. She also senses an ill-informed obsession with ghazals rising. She has loved living in India when being queer stopped being a criminal activity. In her spare time she works as a Public Health specialist. Recently she was thrilled by an unusual convergence in her personal and professional lives when she was tasked with flashing masturbation slogans at a queer rock concert, to promote good safe sex. She thanks D for the original erotic charge for this short story – when it was set elsewhere.

Chicu lives on a farm in the Himalayas with her husband. She defines herself as a natural resource manager, traveller, and gardener. A civil engineer by training, she works in the non-profit sector for the equitable distribution of water resources. For her, reading and writing is a way to understand things that are too difficult to comprehend otherwise.

D'Lo is a queer Tamil Sri L.A.nkan-American, political theatre artist/writer, director, comedian and music producer. D'Lo has performed and/or facilitated performance and writing workshops extensively in the US, Canada, UK, Germany, Sri Lanka and India. D'Lo holds a BA from UCLA in Ethnomusicology and is a graduate of New York's School of Audio Engineering. D'Lo's work has been published in various anthologies and academic journals, most recently: *Desi Rap: Hip Hop and South Asia America* and *Experiments in a Jazz Aesthetic* (co-edited by Sharon Bridgforth). Aside from touring the university/college circuit with *D'FaQTo Life* (pronounced *defacto*), D'Lo tours *Ramble-Ations: A One D'Lo Show* (dir. Adelina Anthony). D'Lo is currently working on his latest solo show *Minor D'Tales*, is internationally touring his full-length stand-up storytelling show D'FunQT (pronounced *defunct*) and is in workshop production for his second full-length play, *Boys that Pray*. www.dlocokid.com

Devdutt Pattanaik writes and lectures extensively on the relevance of myth and mythology in modern times. This story is based on a sub-plot of his earlier work, *The Pregnant King* (Penguin India, 2009), that never made it to the final draft. www.devdutt.com

Doabi is a daughter of Punjab, born from between the legs of the Beas and Sutlej. She is an activist, researcher, writer and an RJ. She works on issues of migration, gender, sexuality and labour.

Ellen L.R. has loved women from as far back as she can remember – from when she was eight years old in the 1980s in Sri Lanka. She was brought up in a more or less traditional Sri Lankan family which, taking its cue from wider cultural beliefs, carefully shielded children from any knowledge of sex, out of embarrassment and the belief that it would corrupt them. Sex was hard to write about, not surprisingly, even after many years living autonomously. This is Ellen's first attempt at it.

Iravi is an occasional writer and a sometimes poet who would love to dabble oftener in fiction and several kinds of wordplay, were it not for her arthritic knee and many other equally lame excuses. She is also a proud member of a queer feminist collective that celebrates words even as it engages in actions and campaigns.

Michael Malik G. spent his early years in New York and first settled in India in 1980. He attended Cathedral School in Mumbai and continued his studies in the United States at Tufts University and Hunter College. In his second youth he resettled in India, in 2007, choosing Delhi, city of unsparing desire, as home and master. He teaches language and literature.

Msbehave is more concerned about canine behaviour rather than her own. She likes to get her hands dirty muddling mint, coiling clay and ripping rubber on the road. Writing, travel, photography and food keep her out of mischief on many a day.

Nikhil Yadav teaches English literature at Delhi University. Writing is for him what perhaps doodling in the margins is for his bored students. He is currently working on a collection of short stories.

Feline lover, erotica painter, city interlocutor, swing singer and lover of all things delectable and eccentric, is how **Nilofer's** cats sum her up. An artist, cartoonist and graphic designer, her work explores the theme of sexuality, both earthly and divine.

Professionally, she designs websites and can be reached at bluinker.wordpress.com

In a world where the categories of 'Man' and 'Woman' exist, **Satya** is a Transman. He is also a gender activist who divides his working life between Trans* activism, cinematography and running a home. He founded and continues to facilitate Sampoorna, a network of Trans* Indians. His writing has appeared in *Himal Southasian*, *Because I Have a Voice* (Yoda Press, 2005), and online at Kafila, TARSHI, and TransAdda. He can be reached at sampoornaindia@yahoo.com.

Vinaya Nayak lives in Bangalore and has taken time off from academics and teaching to stay home with her two-year-old daughter. She writes when her baby naps.

Acknowledgements

Meenu and Shruti would both like to thank Shalini Krishan, editor at Tranquebar Press, without whom this book would not have seen fruition. Thank you for those initial conversations. And once the book began to take shape, thank you for making the process of publishing super smooth for us first timers.

A special thank you to Shikha and Shalini Mahajan for vetting what we wrote and giving insightful suggestions. And a grateful tip of the hat from all of us to Elakshi Kumar for making the title and cover work out when things were dire.

I would like to thank all my feminist friends and colleagues for their enthusiasm and support and for the wonderful conversations that ensued. I can't thank Shruti enough, for being super-patient with many of my garbled ideas and also for making my 'dry' words better.

– **Meenu**

I embarked on a journey with feminist friends eight years ago. You changed my life and it is largely because of you that I have the courage to take on an endeavour such as this book. I reserve a special place for each one of you in my life and thank you for the unending laughter, warmth and strength you bring. I would also like to thank my counsellor for keeping me grounded through the ups and downs of life. And a warm hug to my brother who has grown increasingly supportive over the years of my eccentricities. And finally a big thank you to Meenu for making this a thought-provoking and vibrant journey. And for reigning in my wild ideas and dramatic words in your delightfully sensible way.

– **Shruti**